**PRAISE FOR** *THE BIRD TRIBUNAL*

'One of the most compelling and unusual stories I've ever read ... it sucks you in ur                                             '
Louise Voss

'Chilling, atmospheric and hauntingly beautiful ... I was transfixed by this book' Amanda Jennings

'Intriguing ... enrapturing' Sarah Hilary

'A beautifully written story set in a captivating landscape that keeps you turning the pages' Sarah Ward

'A taut and compulsive story of obsession and control, and of fears real and imagined. Intense and beautifully written, the book is cut through with a sense of creeping dread; Sigurd Bagge is a colossus of a character, one you cannot tear your eyes away from. A masterclass in suspense and delayed terror, reading it felt like I was driving at top speed towards a cliff edge – and not once did I want to take my foot off the pedal' Rod Reynolds

'An eerie Norwegian psychological thriller with claustrophobic unease that seeps out of every page, *The Bird Tribunal* isn't just about the words on the page, but also what's between the lines, with a flood of emotions bubbling under the surface. I read most of the book in one sitting, unable to tear myself away from the powerful emotional pull of the haunting prose. I was aware of my heart pounding, actually holding my breath in places, and an unsettling tingling sensation on my skin' Off-the-Shelf Books

'One of the most unsettling books I've read in a long time ... menacing, chilling and threatening in equal measure. Every turn of the page brings the reader closer to the unexpectedly gripping finale, which will leave you breathless. Disturbing, cold and completely unnerving, I could not put it down. All the stars. Exceptional!' Bibliophile Book Club

## ABOUT THE AUTHOR

Agnes Ravatn (b. 1983) is an author and columnist. She made her literary debut with the novel *Week 53* (*Veke 53*) in 2007. Since then she has written three critically acclaimed and award-winning essay collections: *Standing still* (*Stillstand*), 2011, *Popular Reading* (*Folkelesnad*), 2011, and *Operation self-discipline* (*Operasjon sjøldisiplin*), 2014. In these works Ravatn shows her unique, witty voice and sharp eye for human fallibility. Agnes received the Norwegian radio channel, NRK P2 Listener's Novel Prize for *The Bird Tribunal*, in addition to the Youth Critic's Award. *The Bird Tribunal* was also made into a successful play, which premiered in Oslo in 2015.

## ABOUT THE TRANSLATOR

Rosie Hedger was born in Scotland and completed her MA (Hons) in Scandinavian Studies at the University of Edinburgh. She has lived and worked in Norway, Sweden and Denmark, and now lives in York where she works as a freelance translator. Rosie was a candidate in the British Centre for Literary Translation's mentoring scheme for Norwegian in 2012, mentored by Don Bartlett.

Visit her at rosiehedger.com or on Twitter @rosie_hedger

# The Bird Tribunal

Agnes Ravatn

Translated by Rosie Hedger

**ORENDA
BOOKS**

Orenda Books
16 Carson Road
West Dulwich
London SE21 8HU
www.orendabooks.co.uk

First published in Norwegian as *Fugletribunalet*, 2013. This edition published by Orenda Books in 2016

Reprinted 2017

ISBN 978-1-910633-35-9

Typeset in Garamond by MacGuru Ltd
Printed and bound by CPI Group (UK) Ltd, Croydon CR0 4YY

This book has been translated with a financial support from NORLA.

**NORLA**

NORWEGIAN LITERATURE ABROAD

*This book has been selected to receive financial assistance from English PEN's "PEN Translates!" programme,
supported by Arts Council England. English PEN exists to promote literature and our understanding of it, to uphold
writers' freedoms around the world, to campaign against the persecution and imprisonment of writers for stating their
views, and to promote the friendly co-operation of writers and the free exchange of ideas. www.englishpen.org*

**ENGLISH PEN**

Supported using public funding by

# ARTS COUNCIL ENGLAND

SALES & DISTRIBUTION

*In the UK and elsewhere in Europe*:
Turnaround Publisher Services
Unit 3, Olympia Trading Estate
Coburg Road,
Wood Green
London
N22 6TZ
www.turnaround-uk.com

*In the USA and Canada*:
Trafalgar Square Publishing
Independent Publishers Group
814 North Franklin Street
Chicago, IL 60610
USA
www.ipgbook.com

*In Australia and New Zealand*:
Affirm Press
28 Thistlethwaite Street
South Melbourne VIC 3205
Australia
www.affirmpress.com.au

For details of other territories, please contact info@orendabooks.co.uk

I dedicate this English version of *The Bird Tribunal* to Marit Moum Aune and Marie Blokhus, who gave my book life on the stage, and who, I have no doubt, will perform the same magic in the movie version. Thank you.

I would also like to extend my thanks to Kjersti, my Norwegian editor, and Eirin, my agent. And a big thank-you to Rosie and Karen, my English translator and publisher.

My pulse raced as I traipsed through the silent forest. The occasional screech of a bird, and, other than that, only naked, grey deciduous trees, spindly young saplings and the odd blue-green sprig of juniper in the muted April sunlight. Where the narrow path rounded a boulder, an overgrown alley of straight, white birch trees came into view, each with a knot of branches protruding from the top like the tangled beginnings of birds' nests. At the end of the alley of trees was a faded-white picket fence with a gate. Beyond the gate was the house, a small, old-fashioned wooden villa with a traditional slate roof.

Silently I closed the gate behind me and walked towards the house, making my way up the few steps to the door. I knocked, but nobody opened; my heart sank. I placed my bag on the porch steps and walked back down them, then followed the stone slabs that formed a pathway around the house.

At the front of the property, the landscape opened up. Violet mountains with a scattering of snow on their peaks lay across the fjord. Dense undergrowth surrounded the property on both sides.

He was standing at the bottom of the garden by a few slender trees, a long back in a dark-blue woollen jumper. He jumped when I called out to greet him, then turned around, lifted a hand and trudged in a pair of heavy boots across the yellow-grey ground towards me. I took a deep breath. The face and body of a man somewhere in his forties, a man who didn't look as if he were in the slightest need of nursing. I disguised my surprise with a smile and took a few steps towards him. He was dark and stocky. He didn't look me in the eye but instead stared straight past me as he offered me an outstretched hand.

Sigurd Bagge.

Allis Hagtorn, I said, lightly squeezing his large hand. Nothing in his expression suggested that he recognised me. Perhaps he was just a good actor.

Where are your bags?

Around the back.

The garden behind him was a grey winter tragedy of dead shrubbery, sodden straw and tangled rose thickets. When spring arrived, as it soon would, the garden would become a jungle. He caught my worried expression.

Yes. Lots to be taken care of.

I smiled, nodded.

The garden is my wife's domain. You can see why I need somebody to help out with it while she's away.

I followed him around the house. He picked up my bags, one in each hand, then stepped into the hallway.

He showed me up to my room, marching up the old staircase. It was simply furnished with a narrow bed, a chest of drawers and a desk. It smelled clean. The bed had been made up with floral sheets.

Nice room.

He turned without replying, bowing his head and stepping out of the room, then nodded towards my bathroom and walked down the stairs, without indicating what was through the other door on the landing.

I followed close behind him, out of the house and around the corner, across the garden and over to the small tool shed. The wooden door creaked as he opened it and pointed at the wall: rake, shovel, crowbar.

For the longer grass you'll need the scythe, if you know how to use it.

I nodded, swallowing.

You'll find most of what you need in here. Garden shears and the like, he continued. It would be good if you could neaten up the hedge. Tell me if there's anything else you need and I'll see that you get the money to buy it.

He didn't seem particularly bothered about making eye contact with me as he spoke. I was the help; it was important to establish a certain distance from the outset.

Were there many responses to your advertisement? I asked, the question slipping out.

He cast me a fleeting glance from under the dark hair that fell over his forehead.

Quite a few.

His arrogance seemed put on. But I kept my thoughts to myself: I was his property now – he could do as he liked.

We continued making our way around the house and down into the garden, past the berries and fruit trees by the dry stone wall. The air was crisp and bracing, infused with the scent of damp earth and dead grass. He straddled a low, wrought-iron gate and turned back to look at me.

Rusted shut, he said, maybe you can do something about it.

I stepped over the gate and followed him. Steep stone steps led from the corner of the garden down to the fjord. I counted the steps on my way down: one hundred exactly. We arrived at a small, stone jetty with a run-down boathouse and a boat landing to its right. The rock walls of the fjord formed a semicircle around us, shielding the jetty from view on both sides. It reminded me of where I had first learned to swim almost thirty years before, near my parents' friends' summer house on a family holiday.

It's so beautiful out here.

I'm thinking about knocking down the boathouse one of these days, he said, facing away from me. The breeze from the fjord ruffled his hair.

Do you have a boat?

No, he replied, curtly. Well. There's not much for you to be getting on with down here. But now you've seen it, in any case.

He turned around and started making his way back up the steps.

His bedroom was on the ground floor. He motioned towards the closed door, just past the kitchen and living room and presumably facing out onto the garden. He accessed his workroom through his bedroom, he told me.

I spend most of my time in there. You won't see much of me, and I'd like as few interruptions as possible.

I gave one deliberate nod, as if to demonstrate that I grasped the significance of his instructions.

I don't have a car, unfortunately, but there's a bicycle with saddle-bags. The shop is two kilometres north, just along the main road. I'd like breakfast at eight o'clock: two hard-boiled eggs, pickled herring, two slices of dark rye bread and black coffee, he quickly listed.

The weekends are essentially yours to do as you please, but if you're around then you can serve breakfast an hour later than usual. At one o'clock I have a light lunch. Dinner is at six, followed by coffee and brandy.

After reeling off his requirements he disappeared into his work-room, and I was left in peace to acquaint myself with the kitchen. Most of the utensils were well used but still in good shape. I opened drawers and cupboard doors, trying to make as little noise as possible all the while. In the fridge I found the cod fillet that we were to share for dinner that evening.

The tablecloths lay folded in the bottom kitchen drawer, I picked one out and smoothed it over the kitchen table before setting two places as quietly as possible.

At six o'clock on the dot he emerged from his bedroom, pulled out a chair and took a seat at the head of the table. He waited. I placed the dish containing the fish in the middle of the table, then put the bowl of potatoes in front of him. I pulled out my chair and was about to sit down when he halted me with an abrupt wave.

No. You eat afterwards. He stared straight ahead, making no eye contact. My mistake. Perhaps I wasn't clear about that fact.

I felt a lump form in my throat, picked up my plate and quickly moved it over to the kitchen worktop without uttering a word, a tall, miserable wretch, my head bowed.

I filled the sink with water and washed the saucepan and spoons as he ate. He sat straight-backed, eating without a sound, never once glancing up. Fumbling slightly, I set the coffee to brew, found the brandy in the glass cabinet behind him and, once he had put down his cutlery, cleared the table. I poured coffee in a cup and brandy in a delicate glass, then placed both on a tray and picked it up with shaking hands, clattering in his direction.

When he stood up afterwards, thanked me brusquely for the meal and returned to his workroom, I took my plate to the table and ate my own lukewarm portion, pouring the half-melted butter over the remaining potatoes. I finished the remainder of the washing up, wiped the table and worktop and headed up to my room. I unpacked all of my things and placed the clothes, socks and underwear in the chest of drawers, the books in a pile on the desk.

I made sure my mobile phone was switched off before putting it away inside the desk drawer. I wouldn't be switching it on again any time soon, not unless there was an emergency. I sat there, perfectly still and silent, afraid to make a sound. I could hear nothing from the floor below my own. Eventually I made my way to the bathroom before turning in for the night.

The blade on the scythe must have been blunt. I cursed the drooping stalks of wet, yellow grass that seemed to escape their fate, regardless of how hard and fast I brandished the blade. It was overcast, the air humid. He had gone into his workroom straight after breakfast. On my way out I had caught a glimpse of myself in the mirror. I realised that I looked as if I were wearing a costume. I was dressed in an old pair of trousers I'd worn painting Mum and Dad's house one summer; that must have been fifteen years ago now. I'd found them in a cupboard at home just a few evenings ago when packing to come here, along with a paint-splattered shirt. My parents had bid me a relieved farewell as I had left to catch the bus the following morning.

I started to feel my efforts in my back. Sweat beneath my shirt. Tiny insects buzzing all around me, landing in my hair, on my forehead, itching. I was constantly having to stop what I was doing to take off my gloves and scratch my face. The long, golden wisps of straw almost seemed to mock me as they swayed gently in the light breeze. I continued to swing the blade with all my might.

I'd try the rake if I were you.

I spun around to find Bagge standing behind me. I must have looked deranged, spinning around red-faced and decked out in fifteen-year-old rags. My fringe was clinging to my face. Without thinking, I swept it aside with my hand and felt the earth from the gloves smear across my forehead.

The scythe's no good when the grass is wet.

No. I tried my best to muster a smile, resigned in the face of my own stupidity.

And don't forget lunch, he said, lightly tapping his wrist to remind me of the time. He turned around and walked away. I quickly glanced up at the house, the window to his workroom. He had been standing there, staring down at me in disbelief as I ignorantly forged ahead with my attempts at gardening until he could take no more. Shame crept over me. I picked up the scythe and carried it to the tool shed, hanging it back in its place on the wall. I picked up the iron rake and returned to where I had been working, tearing it roughly over the ground until I had filled the wheelbarrow with lifeless, slippery stalks of grass.

The bicycle was just behind the tool shed, propped up against the wood stack, an old, lightweight, grey Peugeot with narrow road tyres and ram's horn handlebars.

The cycle to the shop only took ten minutes or so. It was a small grocery shop on a corner, just across the bridge, the kind of place that time has forgotten. A bell tinkled above me as I pushed the door open. There were no other customers. An elderly lady stationed behind the counter offered me the briefest of nods as I entered. There were shelves stocked with packaged food, napkins and candles, a small selection of bread and dairy products; there was a freezer cabinet, and fruit and vegetables with a set of scales for customers to weigh their own items.

The shopkeeper's eagle-eyed glare prickled at my back, her eyes following me as I wandered between the half-empty rows of shelves. There was no mistaking her critical air. She knew who I was. I felt a knot forming inside me, tightening, plucked a few items from the shelves and placed them in my basket, every move wooden, my only desire to put down my basket and leave. Eventually I approached her to pay, placing the contents of my basket on the counter without looking her in the eye. She entered the prices of each item into the register, her expression unreadable. Wrinkled hands and a wrinkled face, a small mouth that drooped downwards at both corners. It was just her way, I suddenly thought to myself, relief washing over me, it was nothing to do with me, it was just the way she was.

I raced home, flying along on the thin bicycle tyres, with the fjord to my left and the dark, glistening-wet rock wall to the right, my shopping packed away in the saddlebag by the back wheel, cars passing me on the road that connected the two neighbouring towns. I hurtled down the steep driveway through the forest before stopping my bicycle by the wood stack, crunching over the gravel, opening the door into the hallway and making my way through the house.

Something wasn't right about this place; it was home to a married couple, yet the garden was a neglected mess, they owned no car and he locked himself in his workroom all day long. His wife away like this. I put the shopping away and started preparing dinner.

It felt impossible to move. My body was as stiff and leaden as the rusted wrought-iron gate. For a long while I lay and gazed up at the knots in the wooden ceiling planks before finally managing to roll myself across the mattress and down onto the floor. Ridiculous. When had I last done any kind of manual labour? Never, that's when; or at least not until deciding to rake grass and dig away at solid earth for hours on end.

I staggered without a smidgen of grace between the kitchen and the table as I served his breakfast. Shame coursed through me; I knew that my ungainly hobbling vexed him. As I went to pour his coffee I let out a groan; it was hard to tell which of us was more embarrassed.

I think I went at things a little too enthusiastically in the garden yesterday, I mumbled apologetically.

He cleared his throat and stared straight past me.

After his breakfast he returned to his room without a word. Drinking the bitter coffee in solitude after he had left the room, my good spirits wavered. I had been so proud of my efforts the previous day, clearing the area of dead grass, all the while hoping that he'd catch a glimpse of me in action from his window. My back was so, so stiff.

The following day was worse. The simple act of placing one foot in front of the other was an almost unbearable ordeal, and I avoided sitting down all day long because I knew that I'd never be able to get back up again. My passion for gardening had lasted all of one day. It was always the way with me. I launched myself at things with gusto yet never saw anything through, always started with the same unbridled enthusiasm before swiftly giving up. I possessed no sense of perseverance, no will to accomplish anything in full. It was precisely this aspect of my character – an absence of resolve, my lack of self-discipline – that I had hoped might be transformed. But here was the thing: it *required* willpower to *build* willpower. A more dependable person, that's what

I had to become, a woman in possession of a firmer character. If not now, then when? Out here I had what little I needed: solitude, long days at my disposal, a small number of predictable duties. I was liberated from the watchful gaze of others, free from their idle chit-chat, and I had a garden all of my own.

On the evening of my seventh day, I set down the tray carrying the coffee pot and cup and the glass of brandy, and was just about to step back when he held up a hand, stopping me in my tracks. It was Tuesday. I had only been preparing his dinner for a week and had already run out of ideas. Today: chicken and tarragon. Monday: fishcakes and onions. Sunday: roast veal. Saturday: roast beef. Friday: fried fillet of trout with cucumber salad. Thursday: smoked sausages in a white sauce. Wednesday: poached cod.

Allis.

It was the first time I had heard him say my name.

Yes?

Fetch an extra cup and a glass and come and take a seat.

I did as he asked. He poured coffee into the delicate porcelain cup with a steady hand.

You've been here for a week now, he said, staring down at the edge of the table.

I said nothing.

Are you happy here? He looked up.

Yes.

Would you consider staying a while longer?

Absolutely. Thank you.

You'll be paid after the first month. Does that suit you?

I nodded.

Do you have any questions?

I hesitated for a moment.

Do you have any idea how long there will be a position for me here?

I'll need help in the house and garden for as long as my wife is away. All through spring and summer, to begin with.

That works for me.

He poured brandy into the tiny glass, then lifted it in my direction. Then we should raise a glass.

I lifted my own, and without thinking I carefully touched my glass against his with an all-but-silent clink. We sat in silence. He exhibited no desire for conversation after that point, his forehead creased beneath his dark hair. I drank my coffee and the contents of my glass, and, before he finished his own, I left the table and made a start on the washing up. I heard him push his chair back and disappear into his room as I rinsed the dishes, cold in the knowledge that it was done, I would remain here, yet warm for the very same reason. I had a place to stay, no need to go back. I could live out here in peace.

After a few days of sunshine, the garden was beginning to dry out. I had finally honed my skills with the scythe, too, and now left an aftermath of spiky clumps of straw in my wake. I had started to perspire in the cool air. The pale afternoon light dwindled as the sun disappeared behind the mountains. My back aching, I gazed around me. Spring flowers could be seen here and there. One day there had been a brief flurry of snow, while the next a butterfly had unexpectedly landed nearby. There was no order to things. I dragged the rake through the hay and weeds, clearing the area and wheeling everything to the end of the garden in the wheelbarrow. Dark, compacted earth had become visible beneath the weeds: old flower beds. I hadn't yet touched them, but it was possible that bulbs and seeds and life might be lurking beneath the surface, soon to emerge. Occasionally I would turn around and look up at the house as I worked, and would catch a glimpse of Bagge at the window, always in motion, so it was impossible to tell if he had been watching me or simply passing by.

I returned the tools to the shed, banged the work boots against the wall beneath the veranda to remove the clumps of earth stuck to the soles and made my way upstairs to my bathroom. I filled the tub and slipped into the water, scrubbing myself clean of dirt and earth, uplifted by the new possibilities of my existence. Good, hard work beneath an open sky, the feeling it left in my body, the act of drawing fresh air deep into my lungs. I had never thought change was possible. Not of one's own doing, anyway. Never. The idea that I could transform myself had been nothing more than a notion I occasionally turned to for comfort only to find it depressing when I was forced to acknowledge that I didn't really believe in it. But now this. Committing myself to this: to the work in the garden. Clearing space, making things grow. There was salvation to be found, I could create a sense of self, mould a congruous identity in which none of the old parts of me could be found. I could make myself pure and free from guilt, a virtuous heart. I pulled the plug and watched as the water was drawn down into the plughole. I rinsed my body and hair with the shower head, then stepped out of the bathtub. I heard Bagge's footsteps on the floor downstairs – could he be pure? – then dried myself off, dressed and entered my room.

From my window I watched him head down through the garden, on inspection duty, perhaps, the heavy soles of his boots crunching over the dry tufts of straw, the sight of his broad back as he marched past the fruit trees and carried on, disappearing down the steps to the jetty. I felt a flutter in my stomach. Men, I thought, such beautiful creatures. Some of them, at least. Their voices, their backs. Quickly I left my room and tried the door across the hall. It was locked. I stopped at the top of the stairs and considered running down, hurriedly snooping around; the thought made my heart pound within my chest. I let it be.

His bathroom was to the right, just off the hallway: an old-fashioned tiled floor, an ordinary toilet and a simple shower concealed by a curtain. My instructions were to clean the room and mop the floor once a week. I could decide for myself which day I preferred to do it, he had told me, but had added that he liked to start the weekend with the scent of soap in the house.

As I filled the bucket with water in the kitchen, I saw him walk through the garden. He was tall and broad-shouldered and bowed his head automatically as he walked in and out of rooms. Outside he stood erect in his heavy hiking boots and walked slowly, moving silently in spite of his size. As I watched him move through the garden in the way he did, I was reminded of the Norse god Balder. I liked to gaze at him as he walked away, to observe him from afar. He always wore button-up shirts, and when it grew cool in the evenings he would pull on a coarse, dark-blue jumper. He was entirely uninterested in me, in everything. Everything besides whatever it was that was going on in his workroom. I tried to rein in my curiosity, to mind my own business, to concentrate on what I was doing in the garden that I had already begun to think of as my own, to focus on the task of meal-planning. In the evenings I wrote lists of what I had, what I needed, what I could cook and how I might best make use of the leftovers. It was the kind of task to which I could anchor the stream of thoughts that otherwise drifted so easily to darker places.

The door to the bathroom cabinet clicked softly. Inside were pain-killers, plasters, mosquito repellent, a beard trimmer and a common brand of deodorant. It surprised me. I had almost taken for granted that he must be on some kind of medication. I caught a glimpse of myself in the mirror as I wiped it down. It was clear that the person staring back at me had just done something that she knew was irrational; it was a look that I had seen a hundred times before. That's quite enough of that, I thought; be pure.

I had been fortunate enough to find a gardening book on the shelf, but the information in it was sketchy, to say the least. It said that the bushes should be pruned before buds formed, but nothing about when buds might be expected to appear. I sat on a stool beside one of the nearest blackcurrant bushes and peered carefully at the branches. I had fallen into the habit of engaging in an endless inner dialogue with myself as I worked in the garden. I covered a whole range of topics. I'd always been sure that, if I ever went mad, I'd never be the type to wander the streets and talk aloud to myself, because I wouldn't have anything to say; but here, in this silence, my hands plunged deep in the cold, damp earth or running along dead branches, I found myself simmering over with chitchat, endless conversations with myself, occasionally even imagined dialogues with others, discussing and debating for hours at a time. I lost each and every one of these internal disputes, listening more intently to my imaginary opponents than to myself, their arguments always holding more sway than my own. Other people had always been more reliable than me.

I started by removing the blackcurrant branches that looked as if they'd died over the winter, and after that all those at ground level. I finished by pruning the oldest branches on the bush. The growth rings on the cuttings suggested that the bush hadn't been pruned for at least seven or eight years, and I found it odd that Bagge and his wife had neglected the garden the way they had.

When I finished, I took the loppers with me up the rocky bank to where I'd found hazels growing. If I pruned them now, they might produce a decent yield of nuts later. Shuffling around the garden and carrying out these little jobs to the best of my ability was a delight, but it also involved navigating a narrow path of self-understanding. If I'd had any horticultural expectations of myself before coming here, these had now been quashed, for I now had to admit to the fact that my knowledge of gardening and plants and soil was uniquely lacking in comparison to everyone I knew. I was clueless; in truth I harboured a major inferiority complex where the subject was concerned. Perhaps I should have shown more interest, but the fact that earth couldn't simply be left to be earth, but had to be fortified with manure or nourishment of some kind, the fact that nature couldn't work things out for itself – these had always been the major obstacles that stunted my enthusiasm for the whole thing. In the tool shed I stumbled across a selection of old seed packets, but the text on the back was incomprehensible to the average person, all about thinning distances and who knows what else, all conveyed in a language the likes of me found difficult to grasp. I memorised short passages from the gardening book, and went out the following day to put what I'd read into practice, attempting to visualise the contents of my memory: Like this? Is this what they mean? I froze as if to ice whenever I was struck by the thought of Bagge watching me from the window, standing there, scratching his head: What on earth is she up to now? No, no, not that one! At first I didn't dare attempt anything more advanced than a haphazard spot of weeding in the recently discovered beds. But now I had pruned the perennials as I thought they ought to be pruned, and I was even considering planting some bulbs, though the author of the gardening book seemed to assume that everyone on the planet already possessed both the requisite knowledge and his or her own tiny arsenal of bulbs, primed for deployment when spring came; I was at a loss.

I raked up the hazel cuttings and lifted them into the wheelbarrow, then trundled over the lawn and dumped the contents with the rest of the green waste. Light suddenly pierced the dark sky, the rays unexpectedly warm and intense. I perched myself on the dry stone wall for a break, the warmth of the sun on my brow, then closed my eyes and turned to face it, my back to the house. Sighed. Perhaps gardening was for me after all; perhaps I just hadn't had a chance to find out before now, hadn't ever learned how. I'd pick it up, it's hardly as if I had learning difficulties, I'd always been quick and there was no reason to assume I was some kind of horticultural dyslexic.

Stay perfectly still, Allis, I suddenly heard just behind me, his voice strangely quiet.

Without thinking I turned my head and looked at him, inquisitive. I screamed as he leapt at me, a pouncing lion, springing at me with one decisive, snarling, crushing blow. I fell forwards, down onto the grass, no notion of what was happening or why, shamefully lingering there on all fours like a dog.

He dropped the rock he had been clutching, took my hand and helped me up, I was dizzy with adrenaline, my breathing panicked, shallow. There, on the dry stone wall where I had been sitting, lay a coiled-up adder, its skull crushed.

I didn't mean to frighten you.

I couldn't utter a single word. My heart thumped as I took an unsteady step back.

We gazed at the adder, steam rising gently from the animal's body, a long, patterned muscle in cramp, only a glistening, wet void where the head had once been. I shuddered.

Not bad, I squeaked, conscious that I was breaking out in a cold sweat.

He picked up the snake by the tail without a word and strode up the bank as it dangled from his hand, making his way to the edge of the forest. I saw him crouch down and place a rock on top of its body. He walked across the garden towards the house, grasped the door handle and was gone.

The evenings had started to become noticeably brighter. I took the bicycle out to investigate the local area, though there was nothing to see. There were scarcely any houses, only the main road, cars whizzing by. The grocery shop was my only contact with the outside world, and there were still no other customers to speak of, only the same old woman behind the counter, glaring at me over her crooked beak.

The house was as quiet and empty as always. Knowing there was another person here but seeing no sign of him other than at mealtimes made it feel all the emptier. I washed the vegetables at the kitchen sink and began making stock with some leftovers. I was out of ideas about what I might make him for dinner the following day. If I had properly thought things through before getting on the bus a month ago, I might have had the sense to pack a recipe book. I ambled over to the bookshelves to see if there was anything resembling a cookbook hiding between the volumes on show, but examining the spines I found nothing. A house without recipes, what kind of home was that?

I opened each of the kitchen drawers in turn, then the cupboard doors. Slipped in alongside the spice rack I found a slim, blue volume that I hadn't noticed before. I pulled it out and carefully leafed through its pages. Recipes scrawled in fine, black script. Beautiful, cursive handwriting describing casseroles, soups, cakes. I pictured her, an indistinct, slender figure standing with her back to me, the nape of her neck tanned, her dark hair coiled in a bun with a few curly, flyaway strands by her ears. A beautiful, mature woman. A queen. Mature, I thought, am I not mature? No, a lost child, that's what I am. I stopped at one recipe, an Asian fish soup, realised that I had most of what I needed to make it and decided to cook a small batch, a trial run for dinner that evening. I warmed oil in a pan and added spring onion, chili, ginger. The scents drifted upwards. I added stock and placed a fillet of cod in a separate pan to poach. Just as I was preparing to lift the fish from its pan and add it to the soup, I heard footsteps, the door opening. I blushed and cursed inwardly; I had disturbed him. He stuck his head around the door; I pretended not to notice him.

It smells good in here.

Just a little soup...

I see.

There's plenty here for you too, if you'd like to try some.

Confounding my expectations, he entered the room and sat down at the table as if in anticipation of what was to come. I grew clumsy in his presence. Hurriedly I slipped the recipe book between two chopping boards, ladled the soup into a bowl and placed it on the table before him. He closed his eyes and inhaled deeply then looked up at me, surprised. I ate my own portion standing at the kitchen worktop while he sat at the table. Neither of us spoke. Watching him eat left me with a sense of calm, a warmth. He devoured every last morsel, then took a slow, deep breath and pushed his chair back from the table. He stood up, picked up his empty bowl and walked towards me, stopping directly in front of me and placing the bowl on the bench beside me. Hot-cheeked, I looked down until he had returned to his room.

The kitchen windowsills were teeming with herbs, which I eagerly anticipated planting when the warmer weather arrived. I had already cleared a space in a small, sheltered corner of the garden.

I worked my way through the recipes in the book I had found, and several times now he had opened his bedroom door, peering out as the aroma of the soups I prepared on those evenings reached him, always wearing the same expression of wonder. We would share the dishes without speaking, him sitting at the table while I stood at the kitchen worktop.

There tended to be a fairly dismal array of items on offer at the shop, but once in a while I would discover something on display at the fresh food counter that I couldn't resist taking home with me. One day I came across a whole chicken, feet and all, no doubt sourced from some local farmer or other. It looked fat and happy, and had obviously enjoyed a life spent frolicking around in the great outdoors. I wedged it into one of the saddle bags and cycled back. Safely home again, I chopped off the legs at the knee joints and stored the feet in the freezer for making a stock at a later date, then salted the chicken and squeezed it into the fridge. I prayed to God that Bagge wouldn't want anything from the fridge that day; he'd told me he didn't want any unnecessary fuss.

He didn't say a word as I prepared his breakfast the following morning. Once he had returned to his workroom, I removed the chicken from the fridge, heart pounding, then placed it on the kitchen worktop and left it to come up to room temperature. Carrots, half an onion, a stalk of celery, I chopped everything roughly before tipping it into the pan. I snipped a few handfuls of parsley and sprigs of thyme, then added some garlic and bay leaves, placed the chicken in the pot and poured water over the contents. The pan came to a simmer, and I skimmed off the fat that formed on the surface at regular intervals. I added half a star anise when it was almost ready, steam rising, moisture trickling down my face, the aromas seeming to erupt as they hit my nostrils, and, just as I lifted the enormous chicken from the pan, he emerged from his room.

What on earth...?

Without a word I slapped the chicken down on the worktop, as if it were the chicken that was responsible for the unnecessary fuss rather than me. He sat down at the table and invited me to join him with a fleeting wave of his hand. This ambiguous kitchen ritual had snuck up on us, and I didn't know quite how best to explain it.

This is a far cry from where we started, Allis. I said three simple meals a day.

He waited for me to speak. His hands rested on the table, rough, not the hands of a man who spent his days behind a desk.

I swallowed. Steam rose from the hot chicken on the kitchen bench.

I was quite clear from the start. I need to be able to keep on top of expenses.

I looked down.

What are you making? He nodded at the chicken.

I have a nice recipe, I mumbled sheepishly.

He stood up, tucked his chair back under the table and returned to his room, closing the door after him. I rose and for a few seconds I stood there gazing at the door, then took a deep breath and turned around, my hands trembling slightly as I prised the hot meat from the chicken carcass.

I served him the breast for dinner that evening with vegetables and a creamy garlic sauce, I had followed the book's recipe to the letter. His chin glistened. He let out a long, slow sigh and pushed his chair back from the table.

If you come across any more where that came from, don't hold back, he said curtly, before standing up and walking back towards his room.

It was pelting down with rain outside. He left the table and brusquely thanked me for breakfast. I wiped the few stray crumbs from the table with a cloth.

Uh, excuse me? I blurted. He paused in the doorway to his room.

I don't suppose you have a pair of boots I can borrow?

Unfortunately not, he replied tersely.

Your wife doesn't have a pair I could use?

A peculiar expression crossed his face before he shook his head.

You can wear mine with a pair of thick socks.

He swept past me through the hallway, returning with the green, knee-high wellington boots in one hand. He placed them on the floor at my feet. I thanked him. After he had returned to his room, I realised that I'd also need a waterproof coat. I knocked reluctantly at his door. He opened it in an instant.

There isn't a raincoat here that I could...

No.

She doesn't even have a raincoat. Out here, I thought, in these conditions. She doesn't exist.

What size are you? he asked after I had turned around.

What?

Since you're going to be working out in the garden.

He waited for an answer.

You've seen the kind of weather we get out here. I'll go into town and buy what you need.

Wasn't it a surprisingly drastic, almost aggressive response? He seemed to be at pains to demonstrate that he didn't want to deal with any matters like this in future, and he was willing to buy me one of absolutely everything I might need if it meant that he'd be left in peace.

You mean shoe size?

Shoe size, coat size, whatever it is you're going to need to live and work out here.

I couldn't think of anything else.

Trousers? he added.

I nodded.

He disappeared into his room and returned almost immediately, pulling on his coat and shoes and stepping out of the front door without a word.

At first I didn't dare move; it was possible that I'd misunderstood, but when he hadn't returned by lunchtime I realised that the coast was clear. An hour and a half into town, an hour and a half back again. I glanced up at the clock on the wall and estimated that it would be at least an hour before he returned. My first impulse was to try the bedroom door. My heart was beating so fiercely that I felt my eardrums bulge with each pulsation as I pushed the handle and felt the door ease open. Paling at the thought of him returning home unexpectedly, I quickly leapt over the threshold – a bed against the wall to the right, neatly made-up, a chair, another door across the room. I tiptoed over and tried the door, locked, my curiosity so intense that I felt sick at the thought of what lay beyond it. Constantly convinced I was hearing things, I backed out of the bedroom and closed the door behind me, but was gripped by a sudden fear that he might have scattered a layer of dust across the room to check for tracks upon his return, so I opened the door again, crouching down to see if it were true, to check if he were really so unhinged. The dark floorboards gleamed, not a trace of dust to be seen. I stood up and felt a hand on my shoulder – let out a scream! – but it was just the door handle, which my shoulder had brushed against as I had risen to my feet. Hands shaking, I closed the door and decided never to do this again. Wherever I looked I saw shadows, convinced that I'd spotted him lingering by a window, or passing by outside, the back of his head forever disappearing out of frame, a constant dread deep within me. It wasn't worth it.

Back in the kitchen I started to fill the sink with water, but then felt suddenly compelled to return to the bedroom door. I looked down at the floor outside the room and saw something there; crouched down, picked it up. A pine needle. An old trick. I almost couldn't believe it. It might be a coincidence, I hadn't swept or mopped the floor in a few days, but I couldn't take the chance. I carefully placed the pine needle on the door handle, my hands trembling.

Late that evening, he stepped in through the front door as I was standing in the kitchen making a cup of tea.

Shall I heat your dinner up for you? I felt like a housewife, waiting for her husband to arrive home after a long and arduous day at work.

No, I'll have it tomorrow.

As he passed me his shoulder grazed mine, and I stood perfectly motionless, the steam from the tea clouding my vision. Outside the bedroom door he paused for a brief moment before placing a hand on the door handle. Our eyes met. Quick as a flash I forced my gaze to the kitchen worktop and he disappeared inside. He returned almost immediately carrying a bright-yellow raincoat and a pair of boots just like his own, as well as a pair of dark-blue, hard-wearing work trousers like the pair hanging in the hallway. There must be a shop in town where he buys his outdoor gear, I thought

They're waterproof, he said.

I would be a miniature version of him. For a split second I was foolish enough to feel pleased at this acknowledgement.

He piled everything into my arms, and without knowing what else to do, I bid him goodnight and hurried upstairs, as if I were so thrilled with my gifts that I wanted to sleep in them.

The miserable weather continued well into the following day. He had plenty of opportunity to observe my gratitude as I traipsed around the garden in my new raincoat, carrying out my solitary march like a protagonist from a Knut Hamsun novel, a strange outsider making life peculiar for everyone. Enveloped in the condensation that had built up where warm breath met cool air inside the rigid hood, I felt safe, content. Wearing my new boots there was nothing that could stop me, no terrain out of bounds. The jetty was grey and beautiful in the rain, ripples on the surface of the water, a low mist floating over the fjord. The rocks along the base of the sheer face were slippery underfoot, I used a hand to support myself as I navigated my way across them. Behind the boathouse it was possible to clamber carefully up the slope, my feet sliding on the wet earth as I grasped at clumps of grass and juniper, eventually reaching the top. I heard a crunch as I accidentally crushed a crab shell underfoot. There was a good view from here out over the surrounding landscape. I could see a few smaller, run-down boathouses dotted along the shoreline heading south, each of them bleached by the sun, but other than that only scrub, woodland and steep hillsides. It warmed me to know that there were no other people here. The low scrub gradually transformed into a deciduous forest, with the occasional pine tree here and there. Just a few days ago the trees had been bare, but now the scent of tiny, wet, bright-green buds tickled at my nostrils, the air cold and crisp. All around me I could hear the sound of miniature drops falling on leaves, the forest floor soft and damp, roots criss-crossing underfoot surrounded by club moss and ferns. Pine needles sticking to my boots. The bubbling of the tiny stream that ran behind the house. I'd always liked this. A silent forest of roots and pine cones. No footpaths to be seen. Better still, this was *my* forest. The glorious, clear air that I breathed in, it was all mine. There would be berries in the summer, mushrooms in the autumn. I made a mental note of the different species of tree as I walked, lots of birch, but oak too, and alder and aspen.

After half an hour of wandering in a loop that ended where I was sure the house had to be, I came to a small clearing. There were a few brown, wispy tussocks of dead, yellow grass and tiny saplings, but as I moved closer I saw that they surrounded a black circle around two metres across. There must have been a fire here. Curious, I crouched down, my whole body glowing with warmth after my walk. I touched the earth with my fingers. It was a strange place to start a fire. I felt the cool of metal against my fingertips and picked up a nail, holding it up to the light to find it black with soot. I rubbed it gently between my thumb and forefinger, revealing a gleam of copper beneath the outer layer of black. I let it fall to the ground, but as soon as I had done so I caught sight of another, and another again, black nails littered all around.

Back at home I removed my boots and placed them on the steps outside the house. I could see light coming from the window of Bagge's workroom. As I hung my coat on a peg in the shelter of the veranda, I realised just how much I was sweating. My ponytail was hanging like a wet whip against the nape of my neck. He couldn't see me like this, red-faced and clammy, he'd be mortified on my behalf; but as I shuffled inside in my socks I found him sitting at the kitchen table with nothing but a glass of red wine for company, gazing into the distance. I'd never seen him do anything like this before. Was it an invitation of sorts – an attempt at social interaction? I hated walking past him; I could never tell if he wanted me to acknowledge him or not, never quite knew if I should carry on walking as if neither of us were actually there; which was more conspicuous – the first option, or the second? I nodded as if he were someone I passed each day on my way to work. Then, just before I reached the stairs, I was stopped in my tracks.

Allis.

Yes?

My hair was clinging to my head, my ears sticking out. Waiting at the bottom of the staircase I hurriedly tried to run a hand through my hair to make it look a little less flat, but it was fine and soaked through with perspiration.

What were you doing outside?

Just taking a walk.

Fine.

He waved me away.

I bounded up the stairs, like a little girl. He made me feel so stupid and inferior, incapable of making my own decisions. His expression, contrived, always scrutinising, as if to demonstrate that I was his, that he could decide where I could and couldn't go.

I went to bed early that night, a clammy, trembling hand over my heart. I had never had a strategy to protect myself against melancholy, I didn't have the first clue how to defend myself. I was hypersensitive and overly susceptible to all kinds of thoughts, superficial yet destructive future scenarios, in which my only prospect in life was to fall even further than I already had. It would only be ten, no, five – or perhaps even fewer, three – years before my body and face lost its appeal, so until then I'd have to plough everything I had into intellectual activity, gradually regain some respect, because if not that, then what? Nothing but alcoholism and indignity, trips to the off licence several times a week, no successors, no money – not if I didn't get a move on and get married maybe. But to whom? I'd been involved in a scandal; everyone in the country knew I was a non-refundable commodity, not to mention entirely useless as far as marriage was concerned. That was unless I managed to commit to something. Something that could consume me. Something that wouldn't allow me to break free.

Is that everything? she asked as she keyed the price of the coffee into the register.

Yes.

Nothing from back here? she asked, casting a glance over her shoulder to the stand by the tobacco cabinet filled with packets of batteries, painkillers, condoms.

No, thank you, I replied, puzzled.

I paid, picked up the bags and left without a word. I felt the prickle of her smirk at my back as I departed, the skin around my eyes growing puffy, my jaw clenched. I pushed the limits of my fitness as I cycled home, pedalling much faster than I was strictly capable of in my desperation to get away. Could she really be so repulsive? By the time I arrived back at the house, I felt certain. She had finally managed to work it out; it had taken her a while, but finally she knew where she recognised me from. I was no longer just a random intruder, a parasite from the city that had settled in her village, her shop. Finally, she had placed me, and she couldn't let that pass without comment. She had spied my photograph on her rickety old newspaper stand long before she had finally made the connection, but now she had, she was proud and felt obliged to make it clear that she knew who I was. To think that the whore of broadcasting house was buying groceries from *her* shop – Allis Hagtorn herself, the strumpet that had slept her way onto television screens across the nation. The bicycle gave a thud as it hit the wood stack and I ran up the front steps, knowing that my throat was flushed and blotchy as I stepped inside and kicked off my shoes in the hallway. I needed to get a grip but I just couldn't. What now? Would I need to move on, find a new village, a new shop? Heavy-handedly I thrust the items into the fridge, with it all coming back to me.

Bagge appeared from the garden, wandering in through the veranda door, and a landslide was unleashed within me. I quickly turned away, hiding my face behind the open fridge door.

Did you get any coffee?

Yes, I murmured from behind the door, my voice thick.

He came over, placed a hand on my shoulder, quickly pulled it away.

I grimaced, squeezing my eyes tightly shut then opening them and staring intently at the cheese.

Has something happened, Allis?

I couldn't answer him.

Is it me? he asked. Is it something I've done?

I shook my head, didn't want him to see my face, to see how flushed and swollen it had become.

Can you tell me about it?

I cracked. His face softened when he saw my tears, he took my arm and led me across the room, then sat me down in his chair.

You don't need to tell me if you don't want to, he said, but would you like a cup of coffee?

I nodded.

Neither of us said a word as he made a pot of coffee, I felt ashamed of the embarrassment I must be causing him. He poured me a cup and sat down at the table, facing out onto the garden. It was clear that I could talk to him if I wanted to, but that I didn't have to say anything if I preferred. More than anything I wanted him to know that it had nothing to do with him, that it wasn't the weight of my loneliness causing problems; quite the contrary, in fact. But when I finished my coffee I wandered over to the sink and washed my cup, uttering nothing more than a mumbled thank-you. I made my way up to my room and left him sitting at the table.

On brighter days I would hang the laundry out to dry on the clothes rack in the garden. I was always careful to hang our clothes separately. Today, with the weather not quite good enough to hang anything outside, I had hung his clothing from the rickety drying rack in his bathroom and my own clothing up in my room, where I had pinned a few lines from the ceiling to the best of my ability. Even so, inside the washing machine our underwear swirled around in close contact, tangling together in warm soapy water once each week, and I wondered if he took for granted the fact that I did it like this, the most natural way, or if he'd keel over or see red at the whole idea.

Drying on the lines in my bedroom, in the moonlight my clothes cast human-like silhouettes on the wall and ceiling, and when I woke I was forced to acknowledge that I'd had an erotic dream. As far as I could remember, it had been a long time since that had happened. Perhaps it had been my mind's way of protecting me: There, that's the way, Allis, we're cordoning off that space. No more erotic revelations for you, not for a good long while – after all, it's hardly your forte.

When I served him his breakfast, I found myself caught in a vicious circle – my fear that the unprecedented activity in my subconscious was obvious to see made my body language all the more revealing, which only served to reinforce the notion that even my facial expression alone was giving a detailed account of the dream itself. As I poured his coffee I was paralysed by the thought of my breast accidentally brushing up against his cheek. It was a complete physical impossibility, yet still the thought made me blush, and though he said nothing, I sensed Bagge's faint exasperation.

He chewed his food slowly as I filled the sink with water. I accidentally added far too much washing up liquid and watched as bubbles overflowed in the most vulgar fashion, water splashing onto my t-shirt, like some sort of misguided suggestive invitation. I did my best not to lean over invitingly, squeezing my legs together tightly as I stood washing the glasses, stiff as a plank.

Is there something wrong with your back?

I'm just a little achy.

He placed his knife down on his plate and pushed his chair back from the table, then thanked me for the meal and disappeared into his room. My face flushed intensely as I slowly shook my head and pulled the plug from the plughole. I'd been considering working on the flowerbeds today, but I didn't want to be seen sashaying around the garden like some sort of failed vagrant, hunched over the earth. I pulled the recipe book from the kitchen cupboard and took a seat at the table, leafing through the pages of fine, gently sloping script at a leisurely pace.

He emerged from his room an hour later and swept past me, stopping outside his bathroom door and turning to face me. His hair looked damp, which surprised me – he'd just stepped out of his workroom. Even so, I still felt embarrassed after what had happened at breakfast and did my best not to catch his eye.

I need you to make more of an effort in the garden, Allis. You can't just sit inside all day.

I was planning on heading out there this afternoon.

It's forecast to be warm from now on, I'm worried things are going to sprout at such a rate that they get out of hand, he remarked, then stepped into the bathroom.

I hate you, I thought. What *is* he? Why such an obsession with the garden? That wife of his certainly has quite the hold over him.

The soles of my feet skimmed the surface of the water. I couldn't hold out any longer. I had opened the desk drawer, hands unsteady after weeks of withdrawal, and had turned on the phone. With an uneasy gnawing sensation in my stomach I had dialled the number. What if telephone enquiries were just a hoax, what if I was the only idiot who believed it was actually true that you could call up and ask them about anything – the price of milk, an unknown capital city, anything that crossed your mind?

Yes, I have it here: the first of January 1969, the man at the end of the line replied.

1969?

That's right.

I didn't dare ask anything else, but simply thanked him and hung up. Forty-four years old. What had driven a forty-four-year-old man to live such a solitary, settled existence, almost like a leper, no contact with the outside world beyond that he had with me? A noise behind me caused me to jump and I quickly turned around to find him standing just a few steps above where I was sitting on the jetty.

I, eh, I ... I said, clasping the phone in my hand, my insides swirling.

I just wanted to let you know, he began, walking the final few steps towards me on the jetty, that I have to take a trip into town. I won't be back until this evening, so you needn't worry about preparing anything for dinner.

I nodded.

But do make yourself something, of course.

Of course.

He turned and marched purposefully back up the steps. I remained where I was, sitting on the jetty, until I was certain that he was gone, then made my way up to the house. It was two o'clock. I didn't know quite what to do with myself. I found a book and took it up to my room, leafing half-heartedly through the pages, then went back down-stairs to fetch another. I was restless. The garden was sunny, and Bagge had left the garden chairs out, just under the cherry tree. In a moment of irresistible, unhampered freedom, I found myself heading down the stairs leading to the cellar, where I selected a bottle of white wine, took it back up into the garden with me and proceeded to uncork it. I sipped the wine in the balmy afternoon sunshine, then undressed from the waist up, every bird call or crunching snap of dry twigs in the forest causing me to lurch upwards, hurriedly covering my modesty once again. I felt a rushing sensation in my ears, heard my own breath as it rattled in my throat, I was restored, alert, keenly aware of everything around me. I poured myself some more wine.

I awoke to find him sitting in the chair beside my own. Just how long he had been sitting there I had no way of knowing. I had draped my top over my stomach and breasts, the material flimsy, my arms bare. I leapt up and tried to force my arms into the sleeves, to pull it over my head, to conceal my unworthy white flesh. Bagge stared into the distance, no doubt to save my blushes, wearing the same expression of worry and mild scepticism as always, the same knitted brow. He nodded at the empty bottle of wine lying on the grass between our chairs.

I'll be deducting that from your next pay packet, he said.

Of course, I mumbled, I'm sorry.

He looked at me sternly. Then his expression suddenly changed. He grinned.

I'm only teasing.

He stood up and walked off. I pulled on my t-shirt and started getting up to follow him, out of sheer habit, before stopping in my tracks and sitting back down. The sun was still high in the sky above the mountain across the fjord, my face tingling pleasantly with its warmth. All of a sudden I heard his footsteps on the grass behind me. He sat down in the chair beside my own and placed a glass on the table beside mine.

Can I tempt you? he asked, holding up another bottle of white wine.

I replied that yes, it was certainly possible. He opened the bottle and poured a little in each of our glasses. An intense thudding surged throughout my body. I controlled the urge to propose a toast and instead brought the glass to my lips, sipping its contents without a word. I stared straight ahead. His profile lingered in my peripheral vision, his chest rising and falling with each breath he took.

Lovely evening, he said suddenly, still looking away.

Yes, I quickly replied.

The wine was cold, lethal, I tried not to drink too quickly. A dry white, it felt crisp and cool on my palate.

May I ask you how old you are?

I'm thirty-two.

He said nothing.

And you?

He turned to face me.

I think you already know the answer to that.

I grew instantly red-cheeked. I wanted to explain, but he stopped me.

Don't worry about it.

He leaned over to pick up the bottle and topped up each of our glasses. For a while we said nothing.

How was it in town? I asked, immediately regretting the question that had slipped out.

The same as ever, he replied, bristling slightly.

Silence resumed.

It's getting cool, he eventually said, standing up and leaving without another word. I thought he might be heading inside to fetch a jumper, but he didn't return.

The half-empty bottle remained on the table. I stayed where I was, demonstrating my free will. The hairs on my arms stood up, I had goose bumps. With unexpected alarm I realised that I was crying. It felt perverse to sit here, weeping in solitude; I quickly stopped myself. I sat a while longer before slipping the cork back in the neck of the bottle and heading inside, where I stole upstairs and turned in for the night.

The morning breeze blew warm against my face as I opened the veranda door after breakfast. He was in his workroom as I made my way down to the tool shed and carried some old flowerpots out into the garden. I filled them one after the other with earth and carried them up to the veranda, where I planted herbs in them and positioned them where they'd be sheltered from the wind. Thyme, rosemary, tarragon. Parsley and lovage. When I was finished, I made my way down to the jetty. Halfway down the steps I saw that he was at the water's edge, sitting on the boathouse step, his body half-turned away from me. I stopped in my tracks, unable to understand how he could have walked past without me noticing. I was just about to turn back when he looked up at me, and I had no choice but to continue down the steps and pretend as if nothing were amiss, all with a creeping sense of unease. When I reached the jetty, I stood and gazed out across the fjord. The greenish-black, salty seawater rolled gently towards us, over and over again. He said nothing. I felt irritation swell in the silence between us.

You shouldn't come down here so often, you know, he said suddenly.
Why not?
Fleetingly, almost imperceptibly, he shrugged his shoulders.
You might fall in.
I can swim.
Are you sure?
I nodded.
That's no guarantee of anything, he replied, his face turned away from my own.
I'm going up to make your lunch.
He gave no reply. I climbed the one hundred steps and made my way back up to the house, where I started putting together a salad. I roughly sliced a few tomatoes. I was beginning to grow tired of the

formality that he insisted upon. It had started to feel forced. I had been living here for almost two months now, under the same roof, and I was just as cut off from the outside world as he was. I decided to punish him by going into town that weekend. He could stay here and make his own meals for once.

At one o'clock on the dot, he walked up through the garden before sitting at the table beneath the cherry tree with his back to me. I made my way over to open the veranda door, inquisitive.

I'll have my lunch out here, he announced without turning around. With a glass of white wine.

The table wobbled as I set down his plate and cutlery and poured his wine. He bowed his head, a deep nod of thanks, as if he were mocking me. Silently I stood behind him and stared intently at his broad shoulders. He didn't touch his food.

I'm going into town this weekend, I said.

You're well within your rights to do so.

I'm going this afternoon and I'll be gone until Sunday evening.

Duly noted, he replied, and began eating.

I turned and made my way up to my room. I packed a bag, mumbling frantically.

When I stepped out onto the veranda to say goodbye, he barely glanced up from his plate before continuing his meal.

Sitting on the bus, I regretted the whole episode. I rang the bell and got off at an earlier stop, far from the centre of town, and began marching in a random direction, as if I knew exactly where I were headed, just in case any of the passengers on the bus happened to be watching. I couldn't go into town, couldn't bear the thought of people seeing me. There were crowds of unruly teenagers roaming the streets on their way to various parties, tanned and scantily clad.

After a few hundred metres I decided to seek shelter in a hardware store, but in that same instant my punishment came crashing down upon me.

Allis! someone exclaimed, in a tone of surprise and delight.

I spun round, my hand still on the door of the store, and recognised the face of an old friend from university.

I froze before her with what I knew was a peculiar smile plastered across my face. Neither of us dared hug the other.

I can't believe it's you, she said. What are you doing here?

I explained that I was visiting relatives, and in turn she insisted that we go for a coffee, trying as best she could to drag me along to the nearest cafe. I recalled from our student days together that she had this tendency to attempt to override other people's plans, but I held firm, telling her I had an appointment to keep. Clearly disappointed, she asked me whether it was really true that I had resigned from my job and moved out of Johs'. I nodded.

How awful.

Well, it's my own fault, I replied, barely disguising a sigh.

At that she said nothing, her expression frozen in half-hearted, sympathetic protest.

You were so good on the telly, we watched every week.

Thanks.

She stopped and looked at me, her mouth open, not daring to mention K.

And the university? she asked eventually.

I can't go back there, not really.

She shook her head.

I told her I had a new job, helping out in someone's home, I didn't say where. I could tell that the curiosity was killing her – that she was desperate to quiz me further but was unsure how. In the end she asked if my employer needed a lot of care.

No, I replied, slightly irritated. It's just a large property. He needs help.

With what?

The garden, things like that.

The garden? she laughed with surprise. But you don't know the first thing about gardening, Allis.

I do, I snapped, then told her that I needed to go. She hugged me, pulling me close against her rosy-red, Christian cheeks, savouring the thrill of intimate contact with such a scandalous individual, an episode with which she was sure to regale her book club the following week. Then she disappeared, strolling contentedly down the street in her patterned raincoat, heading home to her husband and young children, my gaze lingering on her until she disappeared from my line of sight. It was ten years since I had last seen her, and I hoped I wouldn't bump into her again. It felt like an unpleasant reminder of the past, but I later realised that wasn't quite true; really it was the contrast between who I was then and who I was now that shook me most.

I made my way out of the hardware store and stopped a passer-by, an elderly man who couldn't possibly know who I was. I asked him if there was a guest house nearby and he gave me directions to the nearest one.

The following morning I skipped breakfast and left the guest house at about eight o'clock. I wandered around until the town's shopping centre eventually opened, then made my way into the largest of the clothes shops, where I was the only customer for more than an hour. It was so long since I had last bought anything new. Every item that I picked out I evaluated on the basis of whether or not it would suit the surroundings of Bagge's house and garden. I envisaged myself teetering on a set of stepladders as I measured a section of the west-facing wall in a pair of trousers I had selected, or sitting under the cherry tree one summer evening with a glass of wine in my hand, wearing a dress I had plucked from the rack. Eventually I decided on a small pile of items and paid with a few thousand-kroner notes from my first pay packet.

Sitting on the bus on my way home, I mulled over how I would explain my premature return. But I arrived back to find the door to the house locked. I placed my bags down on the steps and walked around to the other side of the house. He wasn't in the garden. I continued down the steps to the jetty, but there was no sign of him there either. The veranda door was locked. It hadn't struck me until this point that he had never given me a set of house keys. All the time I had been living with Bagge he had been at home, apart from the two occasions he had ventured into town.

I sat at the garden table and waited. An hour passed. I walked back around the house and picked up my bags. I pulled out the clothing I had bought and quickly changed into a light skirt and blouse, the gardening outfit, as I had imagined it. It was too nice for such a task, really; I doubted I'd be able to make it look like a natural choice for the job I was doing. In the tool shed I found a pair of gloves, some garden shears and a weeding fork. I knelt down at one end of the bed and started work, constantly listening out for the sound of his footsteps. I slowly worked my way along the bed, hoping that he might find me there on my knees, bent over, hard at work. But the shame I harboured about my new outfit gradually intensified, until I felt decidedly over-dressed, unnecessarily dolled up. Long-buried thoughts of Johs began to emerge. Here I was, embarking on a new life as if nothing had happened. It had been so easy for me to forget the old and move on to the new; there was something chilling about it all, about how simple it had been for me to take something I had tricked others into believing was a strong bond and tear it to pieces. Dealing in deception, lying to the point that I believed it myself. What was it that prevented me from being faithful? I recalled an impulsive fit of self-analysis early in the winter when I had looked up polyandry – females who mate with more than one male. I remember feeling indignant and rather forlorn to discover that it was only jacanas, red-necked phalaropes and sea-horses that shared this trait with me. What sense of solidarity could I possibly feel with them?

I don't know how long I spent kneeling there, but by the time I had emptied the bucket of weeds for the eleventh or twelfth time, the sun had disappeared behind the mountain and I was freezing cold. I walked back up to the house and checked both doors again. I pulled on my jacket and sat down on the veranda steps. Hunger gnawed at my insides. The fact that Bagge lived a life to which I had no access hurt me in some strange way.

When the evening had eventually turned to night, I walked over to the tool shed to fetch the ladder. I carried it across the garden to the house and lifted it up, leaning it against the wall outside my bedroom, where the window was ajar. I had always been slightly afraid of heights, and climbing the rickety old ladder did nothing to quell my fears. I had to climb so far up that my waistline pressed against the top rung as I reached for the window. I wobbled then managed to throw myself inside, tumbling down onto the floor and bumping my head against the bedside table.

I made my way down the stairs and into the hallway, unlocked the door and brought my things inside. It felt like a violation of the rules. The house was dark and empty. It felt so different when he wasn't there. I stood there for a moment in complete silence, then walked towards his bedroom door. I listened closely, but heard nothing to break the silence. No pine needle on the door handle this time. I tried the handle and the door swung gently open.

Hello?

The room was dark. He had never asked me to clean it. The curtains were drawn, but the light of the moon forced its way through the gaps in the crocheted fabric. Slowly I crept over the threshold. A shirt was draped over the back of the chair, but other than that there was nothing to be seen. Once again I tiptoed across the room and tried the door leading to his workroom. Locked. I turned tail, gripped by a sudden sense of alarm, springing out of the bedroom as quietly as possible, then out and over to the kitchen worktop, where I grabbed a loaf of bread. I cut a few slices which I ate with cheese, standing at the worktop. I carried my bag upstairs, used the bathroom and went straight to bed, lying there listening for the sound of footsteps outside until at long last I drifted off to sleep.

I was woken the next morning by sounds from the kitchen. I got out of bed and dressed in the same clothes I'd worn the previous day. I found him standing at the kitchen worktop spooning coffee into the machine.

My God. He looked up. Back already?

I got back yesterday. All the doors were locked, so I climbed in through my bedroom window.

I thought you said you'd be away until later today.

Yes, I replied. Change of plan. Inwardly I vowed not to ask him where he had been. Shall I make you some breakfast?

That won't be necessary, he said, I've already eaten. I'm just looking for some coffee.

I nodded.

Yes, he continued, I was out. Visiting a friend.

I see.

Would you like a cup? He held up the tin of coffee.

Yes, please.

I took a seat at the table, a bold move. My eyes lingered on the table top as he added water to the coffee machine.

When the coffee was ready, he poured us each a cup and sat down at the table with me.

New? he asked, nodding at my blouse, the one that I had been wearing the previous day.

Not especially.

Without warning he reached over and brushed my upper arm with his hand. Before I knew it, he had pulled away.

Soil, he explained, lifting his cup to his lips.

I turned red. Explained that I had been doing some weeding the previous afternoon as I had waited for him to come home. He said nothing. I must just have seemed dirty. We sat in silence once again.

Looks as if it'll be a nice day, he said eventually, glancing in the direction of the veranda doors.

Yes, looks that way. I was planning on applying some fertiliser to the lawn later.

There's no need for you to work on a Sunday, he said, getting up.

After he had finished his coffee he went to sit outside. I went upstairs and looked down on him from my bedroom window. He sat calmly under the cherry tree, gazing out at the garden from beneath the canopy of white blossom.

I missed music. The only sounds I had heard over the past couple of months had been the distant purr of vehicles on the main road, insects and birds, the faint splashing of the waves as they lapped against the rocks down by the jetty. He didn't even listen to the radio. In his life only he existed, and me, of course, his gardener, cleaner, cook. I cleaned my bathroom before returning downstairs and opening the door to the garden.

Shall I make you some lunch?

I'll just have a glass of wine. White.

I sprang over to the fridge and took out the open bottle, carrying his glass out to him, a restless energy building within me. He turned to look at me.

Perhaps you'd like one too?

I couldn't tell if it was a normal, polite offer or a hint at something deeper, a dig at my careless drinking habits, perhaps.

That would be nice. Thanks.

I made my way back inside and fetched a glass. I brought the bottle back out with me and sat down in the chair next to his.

It's turning into a nice day, he said in a faraway tone.

You've already said that, I thought. I sipped from my glass, savouring the crisp coolness.

Have you noticed the mice around here? he asked.

Mice?

I see them all the time.

Not inside?

No, out here. Wood mice.

Ugh.

We'll have to properly seal up the house before autumn comes around, otherwise we'll have a problem on our hands.

He held out his glass and signalled for me to top it up.

Have you lived in this house for long? I asked unexpectedly, before I had a chance to think twice.

Yes, he replied, since I was a boy.

And have you always lived here? I allowed the question to slip out, low-key, direct.

He nodded. I wanted to ask if he had children – he could do, after all, from a purely mathematical point of view, they could be old enough to have moved out by now – but I said nothing. We'd never had a conversation that had lasted this long before, it felt best not to push things too far.

Help yourself, he said as I finished my wine.

I poured what was left of the bottle into my glass. We sat there for a long while without speaking. I felt as if I should get up and get on with some work in the garden, demonstrate my unwavering loyalty to the job, but it felt so good just to be there, practically glued to my seat. His expression was mellow as he gazed out at the mountains across the fjord, but I knew how quickly things could change. I stood up swiftly and strode resolutely over to the tool shed, fetching the weeding bucket. I marched past him with purpose and stopped at the edge of the sloping bank. I pulled on my gloves and began pulling up the ground elder. I forced my gaze to the earth and held it there, pulling out the root and tossing it into the bucket, working my way meticulously along the bank, his eyes fixed on me. A stranger crouched before him, weeding in his wife's gardening gloves. When I turned around to empty the bucket, Bagge was strolling over by the berries. I picked up the bucket by its handle and carried it over to the compost heap, not looking up as I passed him.

Do you know what this is? he asked as I tipped the contents of the bucket on top of the pile.

This? Just weeds, I replied quickly.

He laughed.

No. This, just there.

He pointed at the white, daisy-like blooms that peeped out through cracks in the low stone wall.

I moved closer.

This? I hesitated for a moment. I think it's Balder's brow.

That's Balder's brow?

Named after the eyelashes of the Norse god Balder. When the petals close in the evenings and open up again during the day, the flower head looks like a blinking eye.

He looked at me with surprise.

I only know that because I was so obsessed with Balder as a girl.

Why was that?

He followed me through the dry, yellow grass, back towards the bank.

He was my first love. The first to break my heart, too.

I set to pulling out the root again, growing warm at the thought of him standing behind me.

I don't remember the story of Balder.

It's a sad, lovely story.

Sad *and* lovely?

He brings about the destruction of the world, but that allows for a newer, better world to emerge.

A new world, he said.

I nodded.

How so?

Balder dreams of awful things in the beginning – blood, disturbing omens, that kind of thing.

Really?

The other gods become concerned for him, so they gather in the assembly and Odin decides to investigate. He saddles up his steed, Sleipnir, and rides to Helheim. Upon his arrival he calls forth a seeress who lies buried to the east of the gates of Helheim. He asks her why preparations are being made in the great hall and she reluctantly tells him that they are preparing to welcome Balder into their midst.

Balder is going to die, he said. He was standing perfectly silently behind me.

Yes.

So what happens?

When Odin returns home with word of Balder's death, the gods refuse to accept it. Frigg takes oaths promising not to harm Balder from every earthly creation – fire, water, iron, stone; every animal, bird, snake; every plant, every disease; she goes to each and every one of them.

So he becomes indestructible.

Yes. And the gods begin to have some fun: they shoot arrows, throw spears and stones at him, strike him with their swords. Nothing can hurt him.

And then? he asked, sitting down on the stone wall, our eyes meeting for a fleeting moment before I returned to the weeds. He was so odd. He stared at me.

Loki stands at the edge of the group and looks at what's going on, growing more and more envious of Balder.

Loki.

Yes. He transforms himself into a woman and goes to Frigg, who is also watching the gods at play. Loki asks her if she really received sworn oaths from *all* earthly creations that they wouldn't harm Balder. She tells him yes, but then remembers that she neglected to ask the mistletoe, which she felt sure was too small to cause any harm.

I paused. I hadn't spoken this much in weeks. I feared that I was forging ahead like a steamroller, the wine causing me to babble; but Bagge sat quietly, listening attentively to every word. He had asked me to talk. My voice wavered slightly, I cleared my throat.

Loki picks the mistletoe and goes to Höd, Balder's brother. Loki asks Höd why he isn't honouring Balder like the other gods. Höd is blind and explains to Loki that he can't see, and even if he could, he has no weapon to use. I'll help you, Loki tells him.

He craned his neck, leaning ever closer to listen in. I pulled up a final patch of ground elder and dropped it in the bucket.

Höd draws the bow Loki gives him and Loki carefully places the mistletoe, helping Höd to take aim. The mistletoe pierces Balder's body and he falls down dead.

Bagge looked up, shocked.

You didn't know? I said.

Sitting before me he suddenly looked like a small child.

Balder dies?

Yes.

What happens after that?

The gods are distraught. They can't speak, their once-strong arms now limp and useless by their sides. They stand there looking at one another in silence and despair. Not one of them can explain the weight of the sorrow they feel. They can only cry. Odin realises this is the greatest misfortune to hit gods and mankind.

His throat at the neckline of his coarse wool jumper was red.

I picked up the bucket and cut across the garden, emptying it over the compost heap. Bagge stayed where he was, sitting on the stone wall. There was no more weeding to be done. If I were to attempt anything more complicated, he'd quickly realise that I didn't know what I was doing. I made my way up to the tool shed with the bucket. The sun warmed me. I picked up the broom, crossed the garden, walked up the steps to the veranda and started sweeping, the kind of task that couldn't go wrong. I felt the beams of sunlight radiate through me as I watched Bagge stand up and make his way up through the garden.

He sat on the veranda steps, his back to me, and I moved the broom in long, strong sweeps, trying to make it look like a graceful dance, though failing miserably as soon as the thought occurred to me.

Does the story end there?

No, there's more.

I slowed my sweeping and carried on with the tale, trying to recall all the details.

After the gods have assembled, Frigg asks who will ride to Helheim on her behalf to offer a ransom for Balder, releasing him from the underworld and returning him to Asgard. Hermód, Odin's son and Balder's brother, agrees to go. He borrows Sleipnir and rides away, leaving the gods to arrange Balder's cremation. Do you know this part?

No.

The gods carry Balder's body down to the shore. Balder owned Ringhorn, the most impressive ship in Asgard. They decide this is where they should cremate his body.

What do you mean?

Setting fire to the body on board the ship, then setting the ship out to sail. But when the time comes to move the ship from the land out onto the water for the cremation, it won't budge. None of the gods are able to move it, not even Thor. In the end they are forced to send for the giantess known as Hyrrokin, who rides on wolf-back with vipers for reins. She takes hold of the ship's stern and elegantly pushes it out onto the water on her first attempt. Thor is so enraged that he attacks her, trying to crush her skull, but the gods step in and manage to stop him. Ringhorn is finally on the water. They lay Balder out on his shield and carry him onto his ship. His widow's heart breaks as she watches from the shoreline and she dies, too, unable to face the prospect of a life without him. The gods carry her on board and lay her by his side.

What was his wife's name?

Her name was Nanna.

He said nothing.

I stopped sweeping.

Don't you think there's something beautiful about the way she dies of a broken heart like that? I asked, swallowing.

I do, he replied, his eyes dark.

Balder's horse is loaded on board in full riding gear, and Odin places his ring, named Draupnir, on board too. They set fire to the bodies and Ringhorn sails smoothly off into the distance.

He sat in perfect silence.

So ... yes. I paused. I was on a high, my face almost certainly flushed. That was that.

He said nothing. He seemed lost in thought.

I carried the broom back to the tool shed. When I re-emerged, he was sitting beneath the cherry tree once again. He was gripping the stem of his empty glass with one hand and waved me over.

Can you fetch another, Allis? he asked gruffly.

Another bottle?

He nodded.

I went inside and ran my hands under scorching hot water, working up a soapy lather, rubbing away every trace of earth, splashing my face to wash the sweat from my brow. My arms and legs trembled as I selected a bottle from the fridge. When I returned to the garden, he was lying on the grass. Tentatively I stood behind him.

Have you ever tried lying down like this? His voice was distant, almost as if he weren't really talking to me. Warily I lay down, two metres or so from him. The grass tickled my neck.

I think I ought to put on some laundry. It's a good day for drying washing out here.

But there's no breeze, Allis.

He rolled up his shirt sleeves. My entire body was tensed; I was afraid he'd hear my heart pounding. After a while I carefully turned my head just enough that I could see him out of the corner of my eye. He looked as if he were sleeping. His chest rose and fell steadily. I turned my head a little further, examining his face. He had fine lines around his eyes. His hair curled slightly just by his ears. He looked no older than he was. I felt an urge to stroke his brow. He was glistening with sweat. I turned away from him once again and closed my eyes. I couldn't relax, but still I lay there, trying my best to breathe calmly. The bottle of wine I had brought out was on the table, getting warm. I was beginning to feel tired. He always ensured I was lagging behind him, dominated by his temperament. He allowed himself to be driven by impulse. Left me feeling despondent and alone. He took deep breaths, yet hardly made a single sound.

After a short while I stood up, taking care to move quietly, then strolled over to the tool shed to see if there were any mouse traps. I couldn't see any. I took a walk around the house to check for gaps between the frames or around the cellar window. No mouse would be capable of chewing through the high foundation wall. I recalled my father screwing metal fittings along the bottom of the doors in our cabin. I decided to buy some early that week, and to remove the shrubbery that lined the walls of the house to make sure the mice had nothing to climb up.

I glanced over at him, still lying on the grass. It was strange the way he had fallen asleep like that, so suddenly, right in the middle of the day. The wine and the sunshine had probably made him drowsy. I made my way into the kitchen and started on dinner.

When everything was ready and I walked out onto the veranda to call Bagge in, I saw that it had started to rain. He lay there in the drizzle, perfectly at peace. I had no idea what to think. I stood on the veranda and stared at him. The rain began to beat down harder and the drops grew heavier. There was a downpour on the way. I ran out to him. His hair was dripping wet, his shirt and trousers clinging to his body. He still lay with his eyes closed. I shook him by the shoulder and his eyes shot open, he looked straight at me, his expression grave. His dark hair stuck to his forehead. Droplets splashed against his high cheekbones, his lips.

My God, you can't just lie here like this.

He continued to gaze at me, raindrops hammering against his face. He grimaced, then started laughing.

Come into the house, I said firmly, grabbing his hand. He hoisted himself up and followed me up onto the veranda and into the house.

Get yourself changed before you catch a cold.

All of a sudden I heard a rumble of thunder outside. He looked at me.

Go on, go and change into some dry clothes! I nudged him in the direction of his room.

Are you afraid of thunderstorms? He stuttered slightly.

No.

He made his way to his bedroom, re-emerging soon after. He'd changed into a lightweight, green woollen jumper and a pair of dark trousers. I had laid the table for him as I waited. He took a seat, seeming a little embarrassed. I served him his veal cutlet and asked what he'd like to drink. Red wine, he replied.

When I returned from the cellar with a bottle he was still at the table, shaking with the cold. I hurriedly found him a blanket, which I wrapped tightly around his shoulders. It felt like such an intimate act. He laughed at me.

What's so funny? You'll catch your death. I'm going to light the fire.

I crouched down and stacked the wood in the fireplace as he ate. I heard his teeth clattering against the cutlery.

Now I understand why you need someone here to look after you, I remarked as the wood began to burn.

He smiled. I sat down and poured some wine into his glass. He looked down and continued eating. Lightning flashed outside, and after a few seconds a new roll of thunder boomed.

Not far from here.

He said nothing.

You should have dried your hair properly.

Slowly he chewed a piece of meat, wrapped tightly in his blanket, then he placed his cutlery down and drained his glass of its contents. I walked over to the fire and blew gently, cinders whirling upwards and drifting into the room, the flames flickering brightly. I placed another log on. He was no longer eating. The clattering of thunder drifted in from outside.

I think you could do with a hot bath.

He turned to look at me.

Shall I run one for you?

He nodded.

I stood up and climbed the stairs, turning the bathroom tap on and slowly filling the tub. He hadn't set foot on my floor of the house since I'd arrived, at least not that I had ever seen, not since showing me to my room on the first day. I tested the water with my hand to make sure it wasn't too hot. When I turned around to call out that it was ready, I found him standing behind me in the doorway. I let out a gasp of surprise, my God, why did he insist on creeping around in silence like that?

It's ready, I said.

His face was pale, his lips slightly blue. I stood up and stepped back from where I had been crouching at the edge of the bathtub, but Bagge remained in the doorway, blocking the exit. He pulled his jumper over his head without looking at me, he was wearing nothing underneath. I hesitated. He fumbled with the buttons at his fly and stepped in my direction. I leapt aside and turned away as he let his trousers fall to the floor. I blushed, my face hot; what was he doing? He stepped into the tub, his body sliding underwater, his head sinking back against the edge as I hurried out and pulled the door firmly closed behind me.

Agitated and heavy-handed, I cleared the table downstairs. Once again he was at pains to demonstrate just how little I meant to him; I was nobody, nothing, forced to accept the self-sacrificing role thrust upon me. After finishing the washing up, I stoked the fire and poured myself a large glass of wine. I stepped out onto the veranda and inhaled the evening air, tinged with the faint scent of summer, everything around me glistening wet and green. All of a sudden hail started to thrash down. I remained on the veranda and stared at the large pellets that hammered against the garden furniture.

Bagge was probably drowning in the bathtub without even realising it. If that were the case, then he'd hardly be missed. I closed the veranda door and made my way down into the cellar to fetch another bottle of wine. If he could take such liberties, then so would I. I placed a few birch logs on the fire, and it began to make a difference. He had been in the bath for almost an hour, the water would surely be cold by now. If he had added more hot water, I'd have heard the tap running. Everything he did had started to feel so contrived.

God! I thought suddenly, does *anybody* have *any* idea what things are like for me here? I hadn't spoken to my parents for eight weeks.

Hadn't had any contact with anyone, for that matter. Living here was like ceasing to exist. He had drawn me into this, with him, and yet here I was all on my own. Ugh, I groaned quietly at the table top. But there was nowhere else I could be. No other job I could imagine myself doing. Nothing. I suppose I just wanted things to be a little more pleasant here, maybe just to feel more like a friend than a hat stand. Just as my own thoughts were beginning to bore me, I heard him on the stairs, and Bagge, now fully dressed, arrived downstairs.

Better now?

Warmer, thanks.

There's a good fire going, I said.

I can feel it. He pulled a chair out from where it had been tucked under the table, then reached for the bottle and poured himself some wine. He placed the bottle down without offering me a top-up, and even though my own glass was almost full, I was disappointed. We sat in silence.

There was a hailstorm a moment ago, I eventually murmured.

I heard it on the roof. He bowed his head. See? I've dried my hair properly this time.

Yes, good boy.

He laughed. It startled me.

Did you go to university? he asked out of the blue.

Yes, for a few years.

What did you study?

Home economics, I replied, nervous in the face of my own quip.

The merest flicker of a smile.

Humanities.

Of course.

I had wondered if he would be impressed to find out I'd once worked at the university, but his reaction made me suddenly unwilling to elaborate after all.

And you? I knew I'd overstepped the mark.

I've studied.

You have?

He nodded.

Come on, you must at least be able to tell me what?

Law and order. He uttered the words into the air around us.

I see. I decided not to ask him any more questions, it was impossible to know when I'd gone too far. Neither of us said a word for a while. My cheeks were warm from the wine and the glow of the fire. He looked at me.

Do you need to take any holiday?

I hadn't thought about it. I don't have any plans.

It would be good if you could be here throughout the summer.

That's not a problem.

I wanted him to raise his glass, but he sat there, serene and motionless. He can't always have been like this. I hoped that he might ask me to fetch another bottle when this one was finished, that he'd open up a little, perhaps be more inclined to chat with a few drinks in him.

I wondered about applying some oil to the garden furniture tomorrow, if the weather's nice, I said.

You could do.

I spotted a few tins of linseed oil in the tool shed.

He nodded, uninterested. This peculiar dialogue, I thought, so up and down. Damn him. Here we were, just the two of us, the crackling of the fire and a faint scent of wet grass drifting in from the garden outside. I poured the remainder of the wine into his glass. The ball was in his court now. I missed getting drunk. Missed the laughter, the confidence, the lack of inhibition. But I didn't want him to think I was a fool. I felt so young, but not in any positive sense. If only I had the opportunity to say something intelligent. He sipped from his glass. It still wasn't quite empty. He didn't look at me. He inhaled sharply as if he were about to say something, but nothing followed. I wondered if he found me attractive, if he thought about me at all, or if in his eyes I was nothing more than a human broom. He probably existed on some kind of spiritual level where such things were of no interest. I suppressed a bitter smile when I thought about how stupid I had been, buying new clothes, all intended for his eyes only. What made me think like that? Did I just miss having somebody? Was it just the fact that Bagge was the only man in my life now, even though I had not exactly chosen him? Out of the corner of my eye I saw him drain the final drops from his glass. I sat with the stem of my own glass between my thumb and forefinger, gently twirling it, a clear indication that I was happy to carry on.

Would you mind fetching another bottle, Allis?

I bounded out of my seat, unleashed from my chains. Red? He nodded. Red, red, red, I repeated to myself as I descended the staircase into the cellar, slightly unsteady on my feet. Shelves of bottles lined every wall. I had the impression that this was good wine, but in reality I was clueless; I picked a bottle at random each and every time. It was odd that he'd never given me proper instructions about which to choose from the selection on offer. I unfastened another button on my blouse and returned upstairs.

It's good to know that you enjoy wine as much as I do, he said, taking the bottle from me.

It's not necessarily wine I like, more alcohol in general, I replied.

He let out a brief chuckle, then opened the bottle and poured a little into each of our glasses. This was what I loved about drinking, the spellbinding transformation that a relatively simple tonic could bring about, the creation of an alternative version of oneself. I lifted my glass in Bagge's direction. He didn't look surprised, but simply raised his own slightly towards me and looked at me for a split second before bringing the glass to his lips. Together we formed an almost perfect equilateral triangle, Bagge at the head of the table, me at one side and the bottle on the table in front of us. Normally I had nothing against silence, but in that moment I felt almost desperate. A torrent of sentences swept through me, but all were equally impossible to utter. I wanted him to show even the slightest interest in me, I *wanted* him to want to know more; he barely knew a thing about me. What made him want to keep things that way?

It had grown dark outside, but it was no longer raining. The embers smouldered gently in the fireplace, and I stood up to place another log on the fire. As I returned to my chair, I lost my balance and intuitively reached out for him. He reacted swiftly, gripping my shoulders. I let out a sudden, shrill cackle and he let go. I stood before him.

I'm sorry.

Perhaps you've had enough for tonight, he remarked dryly.

I sat down.

No, it's not that, I just lost my balance. I can handle my drink.

Are you sure about that?

Very. I could still feel the impression of his hands on my shoulders, a strong grip, almost too firm. I took a long swig of my wine as if to demonstrate my tolerance.

It's been a long day, I said, preventing the silence from descending once again.

Yes. Are you tired?

No, not at all. Are you?

No.

As far as I was concerned, we could stay up all night long. I wanted to hear Bagge tell me that he liked me, that he was glad that I was there. I wanted to ask him if he found it bothersome having me around the house just so I could hear him assure me the opposite was true, a childish impulse. I held my tongue.

Are you afraid of me?

I almost choked on my wine.

Afraid of you? No, I—

He looked at me, his gaze suddenly dark, piercing.

Perhaps a little, I conceded after a few moments. His expression softened at my confession.

I can understand that. But you don't need to be.

Why do you ask?

No, he replied.

I suppose I'm just a little worried that I might bother you, I said.

He nodded. Well, you don't.

I felt as if something was eroding me from the inside out. That's good, I said.

You are just as discreet as I hoped you would be. He looked at me as if he had just paid me a great compliment.

There's ... a lot that I wonder about, I said, as carefully as I could manage.

He nodded.

I couldn't bring myself to say any more, at least not anything that would fit with Bagge's impression of me as discreet. The ticking of the wall clock echoed ever more loudly. Tick tock yourself, I thought harshly. I wanted to go outside. I could stand in the garden in the quiet darkness, staring into the black of the night and making myself interesting in his eyes. That would give him something to think about. He'd see that even *I* was no stranger to peculiar behaviour, he'd realise he wasn't the only one familiar with that particular art. Or I could just speak up without warning, say: No, that's enough wine for me! Then make my way upstairs without looking back. Goodnight. But I knew that no matter what I did, it would have no lasting effect on him. That was what someone became after an extended period of self-inflicted solitude – stupid and unfeeling, totally lacking the ability to accept the warmth of others. Where was his wife? Had she left him? I realised that he enjoyed having me there, a spectator to his everyday existence. There was no room for any symmetry here; I was just a necessary audience.

I began to feel drunk, the sensation enriched by the silence and stilted conversation and sheer lack of trust between us. I realised that I was impatiently drumming my fingers against the table. He never let on that he noticed that kind of thing. He looked as if he had more than enough on his mind simply processing his own inner turmoil. But I didn't. I was growing tired of this constant rejection. The wind outside had died down, the night sky as black as charcoal.

So, are you in good health? I asked suddenly, alarmed at the sound of my own voice shattering the silence. He looked up at me.

I am, thank you for asking.

His expression was a warning: enough now. My heart thumped in my chest, but I held his gaze.

Marvellous, I said, and an abrupt, awkward fit of laughter rushed free; I quickly reined it in. I had finally become one of them. An awful, vapid girl. Bothersome, pecking away at him. Nothing to lose. Something dark surged through me.

What's your wife's name?

Why do you want to know that?

Won't she be home soon?

Not anytime soon, no.

I had lost the ability to control the muscles in my face, the corners of my mouth pulled each in their own direction. I felt like Loki, an involuntary grin fixed on my face, my teeth stained. I thrust my chair back, swaying slightly, then staggered upstairs.

—

The face in the bathroom mirror gazed back at me, ashamed, the same wide-eyed, frog-like expression I always wore after drinking too much and humiliating myself. It was early. I drank three glasses of water in quick succession and downed a few painkillers. My hands trembled. Bagge's towel was where he had left it, draped over the edge of the bathtub, still damp. I held it close to my face and breathed in his scent. He'd be sending me packing after last night, back off to the city. I took a long shower, dressed and stood at the top of the staircase, listening out for him. I brushed the blueish stains from my teeth, scrubbed my face and moisturised. I listened again. He hadn't woken up yet. Cautiously I crept downstairs and into the kitchen. I made a pot of extra-strong coffee and sat down at the kitchen table. I waited nervously, imagining what I might say when he got up.

An hour passed. I put on a new pot of coffee to brew. Yet another hour passed. He never got up this late. Perhaps he'd taken a taxi into town after I'd gone to bed, booked himself into a hotel, found himself a prostitute for company, all just to punish me. Suddenly I was weeping softly, even though it wasn't all that long since I'd last cried. I held back my tears and listened for Bagge, but I could hear nothing from his room. I allowed myself to cry for a little longer. Could I tell him when he got up, reveal the fact that it was my birthday? The thought made me queasy. It looked as if it would be another bright day. I opened the kitchen door and left it ajar, the air already warm. I am nothing, I thought. I *am* nothing and I *have* nothing. I'm wandering around like an empty shell. I should give up. Stop trying.

I stepped outside and made my way down to the tool shed. Shame. The image returned to me clearly more often now than before, lurching into my mind with me defenceless to stop it. I saw myself sprawled beneath him like a fleshy, Rubenesque Christmas pig, saw him taking me with my stockings around my ankles. The figures in the doorway out of the corner of my eye, their unexpected appearance like a cold draught. No, no. I can't go back, I have to stay here. My stomach churned. I found the bucket and gloves, then strode down through the garden and continued weeding, picking up the pace, faster and faster, terrified of losing my job.

I went back up to the tool shed to look for the loppers and wheeled the wheelbarrow over towards the fruit trees. I started work on the shrubbery behind the pear trees. I systematically hacked away at the dog rose, taking trip after trip with the wheelbarrow until I had created a large heap of cuttings. I continued for hours, forgetting all about my hunger. The sight of my brown arms tucked deep inside the roomy gardening gloves soothed me, brown ankles just visible over the top of my work boots. Working outdoors had made me stronger, more robust. I wheeled the final load over to the heap that had formed, sloshed a little water in a circle around the pile and set fire to the lot.

I watched it carefully, raking stray twigs and leaves into the fire with a slow and steady fervour.

Bloody hell, I thought something had caught fire out here! I saw him approaching through the thick smoke.

I've got it under control.

Do you have a bucket of water to hand?

Yes. Don't worry, I know what I'm doing.

Alright.

I felt as if there was little left for me to lose. After yesterday, it was sink or swim. He hesitated behind the screen of smoke.

Well. Be careful with this lot. I'll sort out my own dinner tonight.

He turned and marched back up towards the house.

Grey flakes of ash floated in the air, the garden waste slowly turning to charcoal. I started to think of Johs as I stood there with the garden hose in one hand and the rake in the other; Johs, who had never been anything but good to me, yet whose life I had still been willing to reduce to rubble, his and my own. And all for the Director General – 'K', as I called him – a man who no longer cared a jot for me. There must have been so many before me. I used to imagine them: pert, firm bodies, perfectly coiffed; scary, superior women. You can't learn to banish that irrational stupidity that lurks within all of us; can't accept it as nothing more than the passing delusion it is, and show strength in its presence. Can't accept that at bottom it is a deep-rooted issue of vanity, that, just as strong as the feelings you have for someone else are your own thoughts about the feelings others should have for you: I am too much for just one person to know! I deserve to be discovered anew: Listen! I love this tune. Taste this wine! It's my favourite. Hear that? That's a little of the wisdom that I possess. Feel! This is how I like to make love.

A puddle of black ash and coal had formed at my feet, a little smoke still rising from the damp. I poured a little more water over the lot and dragged the hose back up to the house. I stepped inside and climbed the stairs to my bathroom, my face flecked with soot, then washed and returned downstairs to make myself something to eat. He was sitting in a chair in the living room.

Are you hungry?

He shook his head. I've just eaten.

I cut a few slices of bread and ate them with cheese at the kitchen worktop as he sat nearby with a book in his lap. As I tidied the worktop, he looked up from his book.

I'm heading down to the jetty for a spot of fishing.

I turned.

There's a rod for you, too, if you'd like it. You do like to fish, don't you?

It was difficult to suppress the wave of elation that rose up within me. I replied that I'd always loved fishing. He stood up and made his way down into the cellar, returning moments later with two rods and a tackle box.

Did you fetch a knife?

There are knives in the boathouse, he said, striding ahead of me and out through the veranda doors.

Silently we walked down to the jetty, Bagge leading the way, a fluttering in my stomach. The summer evening sky was clear and bright.

He picked out an orange spinner for me, telling me it was the best he had. I fumbled for far too long in my attempts to tie the spinner to my line, cursing myself while wishing that I were more nimble-fingered. Eventually he had to help me. I could barely remember how to cast. All the time that I'd lived with Bagge I had tried to cultivate the image of an outdoorswoman, but until this point I hadn't been very successful in my attempts.

Like this, he said, demonstrating with his own rod.

After three failed attempts, I finally managed a decent cast. We stood side-by-side on the jetty, casting out and reeling in our lines, the pink glow of the evening sky before us. I imagined frenzied conversations between us: the things he'd say, how I'd reply, his amused reaction, laughing as he made an intelligent comeback, chuckling at my deflection, his casts elegant and masculine as he watched me out of the corner of his eye, struck by how beautiful and feminine I was, how lucky he was to have someone like me in his life, my rod whipping back up and over my shoulder, sweeping back out over the water, the spinner whizzing as the line whistled through the air, Bagge looking at me and contemplating what a strong and impressive woman I was, and all the while I'd wonder how to bring up the fact that today was my birthday, and when I eventually did, he would congratulate me, moved by the thought that I was born on this very day, thirty-three years earlier, and what a thought that was, because now I was here with him.

So, it's my birthday today, I blurted out.

He turned to face me.

Your birthday? Today?

How can it be, I wondered, that I can gush about that fact as if I were eight years old? What an unseemly, overgrown idiot.

Thirty-three?

I nodded, embarrassed, what on earth had compelled me to say it? Hardly an act appropriate for my age.

He reeled in, then put down his rod and made his way into the boathouse. He emerged a moment later carrying a bottle.

Look what I found.

It was a small, half-full bottle of calvados. He removed the cork with a pop and took a swig before passing me the bottle. The spirit was smooth and warm as it trickled down my throat. I passed the bottle back to him.

Happy birthday, Allis.

Thank you, I replied, feeling small, so small.

He took another swig and passed me the bottle once again.

It's good stuff, I remarked.

Yes.

The sea glistened, pale yellow in the evening light. We hadn't seen a single rise all evening. He reeled in his line and took another sip of the calvados before passing it back to me. It was an unexpectedly intimate act, drinking from the same bottle. He made it seem like nothing out of the ordinary, but that wasn't the case.

What are you really doing here? he asked abruptly.

I looked at him.

Why aren't you in work, why aren't you around other people?

Technically I'm both in work *and* around other people.

Well, only just.

The image rushed back, grey, doughy thighs, I forced my gaze to the water to banish it from my mind.

It felt a bit too early to settle down.

Well, now that you're thirty-three it's probably about time.

Do you think so?

You can do as you please as far as I'm concerned, Bagge said, passing me the bottle. I took a long swig and finally managed a successful cast.

Don't worry about your behaviour last night.

Thanks. I'm sorry about what happened. I reeled in as my face reddened. It's hardly as if your own behaviour was exemplary, I thought.

The sun had gone down; it was quiet all around us. I tried to breathe without making a sound, wanting to avoid disturbing the calm any more than was necessary.

I've caught halibut here a few times, he said quietly. At this time of year, they only swim five or ten metres below the surface.

Gosh.

There'll be mackerel soon, pollock after that.

A flutter in my stomach, I felt a sudden tug at the end of my rod.

I make good fish cakes with pollock, he said.

You'll have to prove that, I said. He spotted the curve in my rod. I felt a powerful drag at the other end and tensed my whole body, hurriedly reeling in as my heart rate soared.

He threw down his own rod and ran to the rocks behind the boathouse, unhooking a landing net from the wall and running back over. I heaved the wriggling fish from the water.

Ready?

Ready.

He unfolded the landing net and scooped up the strong, shimmering creature, lifting it up onto the jetty. I crouched down and placed a hand along its spine as I struck the fish firmly on the head, three determined, consecutive raps with the butt of the knife.

Well, it's not a pollock in any case, he remarked after I had dealt the final blow and we were able to survey our catch.

Sea trout, I said.

Yes. Not the biggest in the world, but it looks good. He held the trout in both hands, weighing it up.

A good kilo, I'd say.

Should we save it for tomorrow or eat it tonight?

We have to cook it now, he said, looking at me with a serious expression on his face. This is the first fish of the year. We'll light a fire in the grill.

He emerged from the boathouse with a board in one hand and knelt down, placing the fish on it. He sliced the abdomen and grabbed the innards, twisting his hand and tugging them from inside the fish before slicing them out. I couldn't look away. He looked handsome with blood on his hands. He threw the innards into the sea and a gull dived down, instantly snapping them up. He cut off the head, stood up and returned to the rocks, washing the fish in the fjord as the gulls screeched overhead, as if deranged.

\*

It was dark all around, only the occasional flicker of light to be seen across the otherwise black water. We ate quietly, accompanying the fish with sips of cold white wine. I had baked the fish in foil with mustard and dill, the embers of the fire still crackling. It was a cool night, I had wrapped myself in a blanket.

I'm curious to know what you've run away from, he said.

Because I'm here, you mean?

Yes.

Well, I am here, that's true.

You are.

How can you be sure that I've run away from something?

Don't you think I can tell?

Out of the corner of my eye I could see that he was looking right at me. It wasn't clear what signal he was sending, I locked my gaze on the black fjord.

How much longer ... I began, hesitant ... how much longer will you be out here by yourself?

You mean, when is Nor coming back?

Nor?

That's her name. It'll be a while yet, she's a long way away.

Something inside me sank. Nor. She had a name; she existed. I didn't ask anything else, in case he clammed up again. I clasped my glass and sipped from it to disguise my disappointment. He saw me and reached for the bottle, topping up my glass without either of us saying a word. This had become our version of conversation. Drinking, raising our glasses to our lips, topping up one another's wine, fetching fresh bottles. I still felt a certain pride at having caught the fish while Bagge was there to see me. I hoped he'd been impressed, that he felt I had skills, could provide for us. I couldn't allow myself to feel disappointed just because his wife had a name. I knew perfectly well that she existed; what was wrong with me, daydreaming that other people's wives weren't real? Allis, I berated myself inwardly, you're not that person anymore. You're someone else now. It was a satisfying thought.

I repeated it to myself a few times. You're someone else now. It's possible for you to be something else. A mild breeze blew in across the fjord, tousling my hair, carrying the salty scent of the sea. I felt a calm wash over me, and that moment, the sensation of sitting in the darkness with him bordered on the heavenly, his low, calm voice breaking the silence only now and then; I almost convinced myself that I could feel the warmth of his body. I wondered what he did, what he had worked as, or what he *still* worked as, who he was.

What did you do before coming here? he asked out of the blue, as if he had read my mind and wanted to beat me to it.

My job, you mean?

Yes, what did you do?

I'm a historian.

Really? I would never have guessed that.

Why not?

He seemed surprised.

I'm not sure.

Hard to imagine a historian without a history of her own?

He gave a brief chuckle.

I spent a few years teaching at the university.

He said nothing.

Early Norwegian history. That's my main field of interest.

Still he said nothing.

We drank in silence. I was tired and drunk, swaying inwardly. I looked out over the shining water, lapping gently at the seaweed.

Can I trust you? he asked brusquely.

What do you mean?

Are you trustworthy?

What, you mean generally speaking? I attempted a smirk, but couldn't quite manage it.

You know what I mean.

No?

He didn't look at me. I took it as more of an accusation than a question, but perhaps that wasn't fair. What is he asking me, if I'm loyal?

Why do you ask?

I need you to be worthy of my trust.

I'm worthy of your trust, I said. I tried to utter the words with a quiet insistence. I turned to him. I am. Are you?

He evaded my gaze, sitting and looking out over the fjord without answering. I am, I repeated inwardly.

I can be exactly what you want me to be, I said, regretting my words the instant they crossed my lips. The statement rang hollow, spineless; it would be best not to say anything else. I took a deep breath and held my silence.

*Kyrie eleison*, whispered Bagge. He turned to face me and stared. I couldn't help but laugh at the way the moonlight made his eyes glint like a cat's.

What did you say?

And *Kyrie elysium*.

He fell silent and looked instantly remorseful.

That would be a nice name. Even nicer than Allis, he said.

Elysium?

Yes. You should change it.

Idiot.

He poured the remainder of the wine into his glass and stood up.

Elysium? he said, facing me.

Allis, I said.

Elysium Hagtorn.

I know what Elysium is.

What is it? he asked.

To enter Elysium? It means to die.

He took a step back towards the edge.

Would you like to swim with me, Elysium?

He pulled off his shirt, letting it fall on the ground and moving backwards as he held my gaze. I sat there, unflinching. His expression was so strange. Like an animal.

What is it about you?

He said nothing, continuing his slow walk.

Would you?

I don't swim, I replied tersely.

Step by step he inched away until he was standing right at the edge of the jetty, then he threw himself backwards and disappeared. I sat on the wall, not a sound to be heard but the echo of the splash he had made as his body had entered the water, playing over and over again in my head. I rushed to the water's edge and stared down into the black sea. A single splash, then nothing more. He was gone. I was almost in doubt about whether he had really been there to begin with. I waited for some instinct or another to propel me into action, but I simply stood there, gazing downwards, paralysed, bewildered.

I— I—! I could hear myself gasping, but I just stood there, rooted to the spot, the same panicked wheezing sounds escaping me over and over, as if I were trying to explain myself: I— I—! my mouth gaping, my eyes wide open and fixed on the murky depths. Hello! I screamed. Hello?!

He burst through the surface of the water with a great gasp. I screamed.

Why didn't you save me, Elysium?

He climbed the ladder up onto the jetty and walked towards me, dripping wet, laughing. The animal in him. Something surged through me and I slapped his face as hard as I could then turned tail, sprinting up the steps.

Elysium! he called after me.

I ran as fast as I could, I had to get away from him before he came after me, before he came to take me. I looked back and caught a glimpse of him, his torso gleaming brightly in the moonlight, gasped and forged ahead, exhausted, on through the garden and over the crest of the hill, into the forest. I glanced back once again to see him coming up the steps in his soaking wet trousers, his dark, wet hair slicked flat against his head. He spotted me. I ran further, on and on, deeper into the forest, my knees all but ready to give way beneath me, to drop me down onto the soft forest floor. I stopped in the middle of the forest, scrambling to gather my thoughts, regain my breath. The forest at night, black and silent, nothing but the sound of my breathing to wake all that lay dormant. I looked back, thought I saw him, hurried through the bristly trees, twigs scratching at my face, tugging at my blouse, tearing at the fabric. Tonight I die. I was forced to stop again, hid behind a large oak and tried to take deep breaths. I stood there, stiff, feeling hands grabbing at me from all sides. My lungs burned, I tried not to make a sound but wheezed as I fought hard for each breath. At that moment an owl broke the silence of the forest with deep, groaning hoots that resonated through the trees. I listened for the sound of twigs snapping underfoot; if he was approaching then he'd catch me. I had no idea how deep into the forest I had run. I froze. He was insane. My cheeks were scorching; I was cold with sweat. There could be animals out here, but what kind? Red deer and roe deer just as terrified as I was, but what else? I started to think about what I might stumble across deeper in the forest. Sooner or later I'd surely come out at the main road, or did the road run parallel? I could keep walking until I heard the sound of vehicles, but there were so few on the road at night, and no houses, nothing. Even if I made it through the forest, out onto the other side, what awaited me there? The very same thing I had run away from. I took a deep breath, hesitated. What had made me react the way I had? I was suddenly engulfed by shame. The wolf in him.

I took a step away from the tree and allowed my gaze to sweep over the forest, pitch black all around. There was no sign of the outside light by the veranda. Slowly I started walking, trying to retrace my steps. Dark, grey, silent night. I crept through the forest, over the dry leaves. My heart was in my mouth. I halted abruptly at the sound of someone shouting.

I'm sorry!

I took two steps forward, listened again.

I'm sorry! He was bellowing the words.

I stopped for a moment then carried on walking.

Allis! I'm sorry!

His silhouette at the edge of the forest, calling out at the top of his lungs.

I'm sorry!

I stopped thirty metres or so from him and stood there, stiff, encircled by the forest, watching him as he rambled back and forth in despair.

I'm here!

He stopped and gazed in the direction of my voice then caught sight of me. I wanted to call out and ask if it was safe to come down, if he was a threat. Slowly he approached me. He looked distraught. One of his cheeks was blood-red.

I'm sorry, Allis.

I said nothing.

I'm so sorry about what happened.

It's OK.

He stood directly in front of me, shirtless. He placed a hand on my shoulder. Silent. I looked down. He let go. We walked down the bank together, shy of one another. He stopped in the garden.

Will you come inside?

He walked ahead of me, in through the back of the house, stopping in front of his bathroom door.

Are you cold?

A little.

Shall I make you a hot drink?

I nodded gingerly, couldn't help myself.

I'll just get changed, he said, opening his bathroom door.

I climbed the stairs to my room, standing in the middle of the floor in a state of uncertainty before unbuttoning my blouse. There was a tear in the left sleeve. I pulled off my trousers, then pulled on a pair of thick woollen long johns and warm socks. My thighs and arms and legs trembled, though my pulse was finally returning to its normal rhythm. I listened for sounds from downstairs. I pulled on a pair of trousers and a jumper and made my way down to the kitchen.

He was standing at the stove wearing a white wool jumper, his hair still damp. I took a seat at the table. The moon was shining more brightly than I had ever seen before, it must have been well past two o'clock in the morning, perhaps even three. He turned to me.

Better?

Yes.

Good.

He took the pan off the heat and filled a mug that he passed to me. Hot toddy with red wine.

The mug steamed gently, the scent of cinnamon. I brought it to my lips and took a sip, the steam making my forehead damp.

It's good.

My wife makes it in the winter, he mumbled.

He took a seat at the table, seemed suddenly timid. This is what life is like for him, I thought. Nothing to prevent him sitting up all night long. He experiences twice as many moods as the average person, the entire spectrum. I peered cautiously at him, trying to judge from a neutral standpoint if I should leave, if he could hurt me.

You think I'm dangerous, he said just as the thought was crossing my mind.

No! I blurted automatically, but changed my mind, forcing myself to look him in the eye. Have you given me reason to think anything else?

He looked at me with surprise, then his expression changed, his brow weighed down with sorrow. I regretted my words.

You just can't seem to behave like any normal person, I muttered, trying to adopt a sardonic, scolding tone.

He gave a fleeting smile.

No, he replied. His black hair shone.

I took a sip from my mug, feeling wide awake. I caught a glimpse of our reflection in the veranda door, his broad, white back, his outline, my own eyes like two black holes, my fringe draping heavily over them.

Why did you come back?

From the forest? Where do you think I should have gone?

I was sure that was you gone for good.

Really?

He said nothing.

I was afraid, I said, smiling apprehensively, embarrassed.

So was I.

I looked at him.

Afraid that you wouldn't come back.

He stood up, fetched the small pan from the stove and topped up our mugs before placing it back down again.

Then you'd have had to come and get me.

I would have.

He gazed at me with the faintest hint of a smile. My head felt warm and I took a long sip. He looked at peace. He sat upright with his hands around his steaming mug. I placed my hands in front of me on the table, tried to relax. His hands, brown and strong. Warm. I felt a vague flutter in my stomach, an empty, sad flutter. If only those hands could just touch mine.

But now it's definitely time for bed, Bagge said, without warning. The legs of his chair scraped hard against the floor as he stood up. He crossed the room, heading for his bathroom, then stopped.

Sleep well.

The tool shed was full of things that could be put to good use; there were broad, light-coloured planks arranged in piles against the walls. They were heavy, but I managed to carry a few out into the garden and set to work. The night's mist had just lifted, and the sun gently tickled the nape of my neck. The illustrations in the gardening book didn't make the task ahead seem particularly difficult, but it might just as easily have been true that my limited skills prevented me from knowing.

He hadn't appeared at breakfast, but now he walked towards me, surprised to find me toiling away in the grass with planks, the ends of which I was attempting to nail together.

What are you doing?

Building raised beds, for the vegetable garden.

Vegetable garden?

Did you need them for something else?

He shook his head.

No. But it's good to have some extra supplies lying around, so make a note of how many you use.

OK, I said. Make a note? Where exactly? He only ever said these things to exert his control over me. He looked as if he were about to turn around and walk back up to the house, but his gaze remained fixed on me. He took a deep breath.

Allis, about what happened yesterday—

Don't worry about it, really, it's fine.

I looked him in the eye to show him that I meant what I said, and I felt sure I saw his brow lift slightly.

I need to go into town, he said.

Will you be back for dinner?

I'll have something there. I might be late.

How late, do you think?

He shrugged. I might need to stay the night.

He disappeared back inside the house and I carried on with my woodwork. Shortly after I heard his footsteps crunching over the gravel, a large leather satchel slung over his shoulder, his back disappearing through the gate.

I had felt sombre when I had got up that morning; so it felt good to lose myself in physical work. It was the only thing that helped – aching muscles, mild, green air in my lungs, the sun on my back. Even so, now that he was gone, my sombre mood returned.

As I carried on working on the raised beds, I pondered how I'd get a hold of bags of soil without a car. I'd need to visit a garden centre. I had no idea where the nearest one might be, but I'd probably need to go into town. I estimated that I had enough materials to knock up three two-by-one-metre boxes.

By the time they were finished, I was exhausted. I left them on the grass and went inside to take a shower. Afterwards I made myself a simple dinner and went up to my room to read some more of the gardening book, but I couldn't concentrate and set the book aside. A combination of alcohol and too little sleep, I thought to myself. My eyes roved around the room as I lay motionless, a restless sensation working its way through my body. Eventually I opened the bedside table drawer and plucked out my mobile phone. I hadn't touched it since the day I had called directory enquiries. I hesitated for a moment, then turned it on. Waited. Tapped in my password. Waited. One message. It was from my mother, telling me that the university and Johs had forwarded all of my post to her, and that she needed an address if she was going to be able to send it on to me. I replied with the address without giving his name, unwilling to offer it up to her, knowing that they'd only start snooping around or turn up unannounced for a visit. I let out a brief, horrified chuckle at the thought of my father meeting Bagge. I did feel a short, sharp stabbing pain in my chest at the thought of Johs, not because I missed him, but because I had left him there to deal with all of the paperwork. I knew I had to take charge and deal with the separation and divorce, but the thought alone was enough to leave me feeling drained.

I went downstairs and found a roll of freezer tape in the kitchen, scrawled my name on a piece and wandered up to the roadside, where I stuck it under his name on the letter box. I did my best to make it look as temporary as possible, in case he caught sight of it on his way back, or, God forbid, if his wife were suddenly to appear. I forced out a nervous laugh, a painful twinge in my stomach.

Two days later, everything arrived. Fortunately the majority of the post I received could be binned. My stomach had wound itself in knots over debt-collection letters for my newspaper subscription and various other things that Johs had forwarded to my parents, but my relief at the fact that most of the mail was about issues quite easy to deal with was greater than my anxiety. How surprisingly simple it is to leave, I thought to myself. Do people even realise? It's not the kind of thing that should be allowed to get out.

I hadn't heard a word from Bagge, and I stalked around the house with a creeping sense of unease. He had said he'd be late, but not that he'd be gone for this long.

The woman in the shop had placed a stand of seed packets by the till. I inspected them discreetly as I placed my items on the cash desk, but I bought nothing, having no desire to grow anything in the garden that had come from her.

You're quite content down there with that Bagge, I gather.

She entered the items as she spoke, never once looking me in the eye.

Yes, I—

That's good. He'd be lonely without someone there.

I paid. She turned away from me and began slicing open some cardboard boxes with a blade to indicate that our conversation was over. I made my way home with an uncomfortable feeling of being watched. How could she possibly know that I was living with Bagge? I wondered if I should mention it to him, but decided it was best to let it go.

When I let myself into the house, it was clear that he still hadn't returned. I put the items away in the kitchen. I felt as if she was purposefully trying to put me on edge.

The letterbox. Of course. My name, taped under his.

I ran up to the roadside and ripped off the piece of tape. A thought sprang to mind: I reject you. I had no idea what it meant, but over and over again the words ran through my head – reject you, reject you – like some kind of mantra. It had been three days now. Where was he? A heavy stone of anxiety in the pit of my stomach, I knew that something was wrong. Was this just a normal part of living with Bagge, or had something happened? And the woman at the shop, what exactly did she know about me? I checked that all of the doors were locked before going upstairs. Lying in my bed, I was gripped with an intense, inexplicable anguish. I was sure that I could hear cars gliding silently along the road and down towards the house with dimmed headlights, voices and the crunch of shoes on the gravel outside. I listened and listened, hiding beneath the sheets, knowing that if someone were to come and take me now, I was enough of a coward to comply without protest; naked and feeble, I cowered beneath the sheets, hoping they'd get it over with quickly, just shoot me in the head through my covers and be done with it. I wished I had the nerve to get out of my bed and pull on the clothes I'd left draped over the back of the chair. I least I'd know then that *that* problem was solved, if nothing else, that I might be a little better prepared for things when they did eventually unfold. Yet I just lay there stiffly, not daring to move an inch, just listening and listening.

All throughout the following day I meandered around the house and garden, dreading the onset of evening. I listened out for Bagge, mulling over what might have happened to him. I tried to do a little work in the garden, but whenever I stood with my back to the rest of the property I was overcome with a fear that I might be attacked from behind. I tried moving slowly around the flowerbeds with authority, but my body was stiff, each heartbeat hacking at my chest. I hummed quietly as I worked with the hoe, as if trying to fool my mind into believing that I was calm.

I moved indoors, it felt safest there. I checked the doors several times before heading to the kitchen to see what I might be able to throw together for dinner. I started chopping vegetables for an oven-baked ratatouille. Courgette, pepper, onion, aubergine, all became fine, delicate slices that I arranged in rows in a dish and lightly brushed with oil.

Without warning a loud crash resounded against the veranda door.

I jerked over into a hunch, felt the stomach-churning, soft sensation of metal through skin, blood rushing from my index finger. I dropped the knife and grabbed the roll of paper towels, wrapping the sheets tightly around my finger and hurrying over to the door, eyes flashing back and forth as they scanned my surroundings, my heart in my mouth.

It had been a loud, hard crash against the glass pane, I felt certain of it. My finger throbbed gently, the blood soaking through the paper towel. I couldn't see a thing. An attack. I quickly moved away from the window and pressed myself up against the wall, pulling my body in as close as I could, my heart thudding fiercely, my finger pulsating more aggressively, a shiver surging through me as if I were about to faint.

Pull yourself together, Allis! I reprimanded myself harshly, you can't go around fainting over nothing!

I took a deliberate, deep breath and stretched my head out again to look through the glass. On the veranda lay a tiny bundle, rust-red and grey. I took a step closer; a robin. I should have recognised the crash against the door straight away, the same thing had happened so many times throughout my childhood, birds always flying into window panes, I couldn't count how many little funerals I'd held as a child with psalms and processions for the feathered deceased.

I slipped on a pair of shoes and walked down to the tool shed to look for the shovel, then pulled on my gloves and picked up the robin, turning it over gently in my hands; it weighed nothing at all. It lay in my hand with its eyes closed, a poor, tiny, lifeless body. I dug a hole by the woodpile and carefully placed the feathered bundle inside. Thank you for the birds that sing, thank you God for everything, Amen, I said, then filled the hole with earth once again.

When evening fell, I drew the curtains throughout the whole house. The reflections in the windows were making me jump; I was constantly convinced that I could see pale faces gliding by outside. I cursed my own cowardice. By the time it was dark, I realised that I needed a weapon to keep at my bedside. I pulled on my shoes, unlocked the door and hurried down the steps, across the garden and into the tool shed. I stared at the alternatives on the wall before me. Axe or hammer, axe or hammer. Defending myself with an axe would be a messy affair, so I took down the hammer from where it was hanging on the wall, closed the door behind me and charged back across the garden, up the steps and back inside. I locked the door and stood there, bolt upright with the hammer in an outstretched hand, thinking for a moment about how foolish I was being, yet just how little choice I had in the matter.

I went to bed fully clothed, the hammer on the bedside table.

Where is he? He must realise that I can't be here without him. My fourth night alone in the house, more afraid now than I had been yesterday. I lay back and closed my eyes.

For a long while I listened to the sound of my own breathing, slowly feeling calmer, then my eyes flew wide open: I could hear the sound of orchestral music outside. I didn't dare move, but lay perfectly still, all of my senses alert, listening. Quietly from the forest, strings and trombones, a symphony. My heart hammered, I wished that I were dead. I exhaled with relief when I realised that I was hearing the bubbling of the stream that ran along behind the house.

Cold with sweat, I took a deep breath and closed my eyes once again.

I was woken by noises downstairs and, having forgotten my night-time terrors, I immediately recognised the footsteps as his. Oh! Oh, God! I trembled with delight, sprinting out of my room and down-stairs in the clothes I'd fallen asleep in.

It's you! I almost screeched the words, unable to keep my delight in check.

He was standing in the hallway. He looked different, his face wan, dark rings under his eyes. He looked terrible.

Hello, Allis.

Hello, Allis? Was that it? I stood there alert, gazing at him, my whole face frozen in an open-mouthed, over-the-top grin that I couldn't suppress.

I was worried about you.

Things took a little longer than expected.

He said no more, slung his leather satchel over one shoulder and headed for his bedroom. Perplexed, I watched him go. I had invested so much fear and emotion into his disappearance, and this was my only reward.

I placed the items on the cash desk, bristling, ready for some ambigu-ous comment or another. She entered each item into the register by hand, knew the prices of everything off by heart, keying them in and passing them along the cash desk when she had finished with them.

Oh, he's certainly lucky to have you, she mumbled softly, almost silently.

I looked up at her, yellow-grey, woolly hair, eyes squinting, the indistinct outline of her figure concealed behind her red apron. She continued tapping in the items.

A bit of dinner will be nice. A bit of dinner with something nice for after, I'm sure.

I had nothing to say. I took my items and returned to my bicycle. I wanted to scream, but instead I channelled my energy into pedalling all the harder. Something nice for after. I felt insulted, but I couldn't help but wonder how this woman, with her tragic appearance and her pathetic little shop on the brink of closure, how *she* could make me feel that way. The fact was I had allowed her to make me feel this way; I was too easily offended. I had every reason to feel insulted by her calculating insinuations, uttered in hushed, scornful tones. Lucky to have me. She might as well have carved the word 'harlot' across my forehead.

A creeping nausea rose up within me as I entered the house and carried the bags into the hallway. Just as I was passing his bathroom, the door opened and he emerged. He looked as if he wanted to say something, but I quickly hurried past him and into the kitchen. Typical, I thought to myself, feeling upset as I lingered by the kitchen worktop, typical for common people like her to pick on others who have made something of themselves in life. Working hard, dedicating oneself to something and finding success, these were things common people always found hard to swallow – it just serves to remind them of their own insignificance. Just one small slip-up and they tear you down with howls of glee. Ugh, no. Working the earth was having an unfortunate effect on me; I had started to feel as if I was some kind of superwoman.

He had hardly stepped out of his room since his return. I had only caught the muffled sound of footsteps as he made his way from his bedroom to the bathroom and back again. He had asked me not to make him any breakfast or dinner until he instructed me otherwise. I understood little of what was going on, but I had no authority to probe. But he had to eat. And wasn't that my responsibility, wasn't that precisely what I was paid to do? I decided to smoke him out with the scent of freshly-baked bread. I knew that he insisted on my buying the dense, dark, bitter, plastic-wrapped pumpernickel loaves from the shop, but there was a recipe for rye bread in the book I'd found that I was sure would bring him around.

I combined the wholemeal and coarse rye flour with the treacle and other ingredients to form a sticky dough. It was only after I'd placed the bread tin in the oven that I spotted the fact that it had to stay there for fifteen hours; goodness me, it was to be steamed, not baked. Fifteen hours. It was five o'clock now. The bread wouldn't be ready until breakfast the following morning.

At around midnight I started dusting the bookshelves in the living room. I didn't want him to think I was the kind of person to sleep on the job, couldn't bear the idea. The loaf tin was engulfed in steam. I was afraid that he would leave his room to find the oven switched on in the middle of the night – it was tantamount to handing in my resignation. Obviously there's no harm in just going to bed, I thought to myself, but what should I do? Write him a note in case he gets up in the night? What purpose would that serve, other than to reveal the time and effort I had put into mulling over the whole issue? At around two o'clock in the morning, I lay down with a book on the tiny couch behind the table.

I awoke to the sound of him stepping out of his room. The bread! I had drifted off. What would he think, what was the time? No, it was completely dark, I had only nodded off briefly. I stayed where I was, stretched out on the sofa behind the table, and he walked through the hallway and into the bathroom. Four o'clock. I considered hurrying up to my bedroom but he could emerge at any moment, so I stayed where I was, stock-still. I heard a faint humming sound, a mysterious thrum over and over again, then after a few minutes it stopped. I heard the sound of fumbling, then the flush of the toilet. He stepped out of the bathroom; I lay as flat to the couch as possible, my heart thudding, reverberating through the walls around me. He stopped by the kitchen door, where the oven glowed like an old atomic reactor, then returned to his room, and just before he closed the door I caught a glimpse of him. I should never have seen what I did. If just one thing in this world was certain, it was that I ought never to have seen what I did. His head was bare. He had shaved off all of his hair. His cranium was white but for a few stripes of dark hair that had been missed.

I heard footsteps outside as I stood in the kitchen early in the morning, preparing to slice the steaming-hot loaf of bread. I hurried to the outer door and peered out through the film of condensation that covered the glass pane, spotting his outline as he passed through the gate and continued along the drive with long, swift strides. Silently I turned the key to unlock the door and gently gripped the door handle, pulling it ajar. I saw the back of his head, so pale, growing steadily smaller as he made his way up to the main road all dressed in black. How had he managed to make it out of the house without me hearing him? The image of him during the night returned to me over and over again, like a knife to my stomach each time, I felt queasy. There might be plausible explanations for a lot of things, but not for that.

I went into his bathroom. He had done a good job of tidying up, not a single stray hair to be found. Back in the kitchen I cut the bread into quarters, wrapping each in cling film and popping them in the freezer. This wasn't right. I walked out into the garden and stood there for a while, perfectly still, gazing in the direction of the road. Nothing. He was gone. I hesitated for a moment then scurried over to the tool shed. I opened the door and brought out the ladder, laying it on the grass at my feet, then filled a bucket with warm, soapy water in the kitchen, grabbed a cloth and returned outside.

I cleaned the other windows first – it would look less suspicious if he were to return all of a sudden. My heart thumped as I leaned the ladder up against the wall on the other side of the house from my bedroom. The top rung rested beneath the window of the locked room. I trembled as I climbed the ladder, it was high. The window was filthy, like gazing into the contents of a vacuum cleaner bag. I wiped the cloth across the pane and moved closer, peering through the glass. I spotted a few boxes stacked up against the wall across the room. Women's shoes and boots. More cardboard boxes lined the other wall, some filled with folded garments; it wasn't difficult to see they were women's clothes. So this was where he kept his wife's things. But why? – Was she going to be away for so long that her belongings needed to be packed away like this?

So she existed. Nor. For a while I had come to think of his wife as nothing more than a mere fabrication. Clearly not, after all. I felt relieved, in a way. If he had been lying about his wife, what else might he have lied about? I wiped the windowpane clean and cautiously climbed back down to solid ground.

I carried the ladder around the house and leaned it up against the wall beneath the window of his workroom. My stomach was in knots. I walked a little way towards the road to check if I could see him there, but there was no sign of him. I returned to the ladder, squeezed out my soapy cloth and climbed the rungs, wiping the cloth over the glass to reveal white crocheted lace curtains on the other side of the pane. I rested my forehead against the wet glass and peered inside. My focus shifted around, but it was impossible to see anything.

After returning the ladder to the tool shed, I felt hollow. The wife who existed, who could return. I hardly dared dwell on it, I couldn't be here when that happened.

I didn't know what to do with myself. Would he be gone for as long as last time? Couldn't he give me some idea of his plans, at the very least? Should I start absconding on a whim, too? I brewed a pot of coffee and took a seat under the cherry tree, which bustled with the same chalk-white blooms as the other fruit trees. The sun danced pleasantly on my skin. A glorious sense of chaos reigned in the garden, increasing steadily, spreading and unfurling with every day that passed. Each and every bout of rain and the ensuing sunshine inspired something new to spring from the earth, demanding space to sprout and grow.

After taking the coffee pot back into the house, I returned to the garden with the gardening book and a pad of paper, determined to approach things systematically and with renewed perseverance. I stopped at each and every plant that I couldn't identify with certainty, leafing through the pages one by one until I found it listed there, comparing stems and petals and everything else that I could see until I could make a note of the species without any lingering doubts, then carefully taping the note to a branch or wrapping it around the stem, or affixing it to a stone in front of the more rambling species.

After a few hours I had looked up almost thirty different species, which left me feeling proud if vaguely exhausted. If nothing else, I had gained a new appreciation for language. In my notebook I had scrawled the names of various plant types: bloody crane's bill, wood avens, St Patrick's cabbage, hairy rock-cress, yellow pimpernel, endless inventive combinations of words. In every bed there was a blissful mix of splendid, solemn garden plants and unruly wild flowers that had wilfully and independently put down their roots. A dense hedge of sweet briar sheltered the garden from the cool fjord breeze. How could I have remained so ignorant about plants for so long? I had lived in the city for years and had hardly seen any private gardens, just the odd, half-hearted communal park. But as I thought about it I realised that I had grown up in a garden. It only occurred to me then that my parents would spend every weekend outside, always working on something or other. With hindsight I saw it all – my mother on her knees by the flowerbed along the wall, gardening gloves on, bucket and trowel and fork to hand. My father's all-consuming composting project. My mother's herb garden. The pots of chives that gave every kid in the local area bad breath all summer long. Rhubarb by the corner of the lawn, gooseberry bushes over by the spruce trees, long stalks laden with pea pods, vegetable patches teeming with carrots and potatoes. Raspberries and blackberries, and blueberry bushes in the forest that backed onto the house. Yes, the forest, my God, I grew up in that forest, it had been where we had spent most of our time, sprinting around in the sheltered woodland all summer long, now all but forgotten. Nowadays the forest, the natural world, it all felt foreign to me, it had come to represent a lack of control where it had once felt like home.

There was a sudden, unexpected downpour, and I ran up to the veranda and waited there under cover until the rain gave way to equally sudden, balmy afternoon sunshine. The weather here could change as swiftly as Bagge's mood.

I crossed the garden to fetch the spade from the tool shed, and when I re-emerged he was there, looming unexpectedly before me, tall and broad. A sincere, boundless sense of relief ruptured within me and the spade fell from my hand.

There you are! I exclaimed, though he had only been gone since that morning.

His leather satchel was lying on the ground by his feet. He stood before me, his skull pale and angular, dressed in his black suit. One hand in the pocket of his trousers, his black shoes gleamed. He glared at me.

Allis, the oven was on when I got up in the night.

Yes, I'm sorry about that, I was baking a loaf of bread.

Surely you realise that you can't just leave the oven whirring away all night long.

Yet again I felt childish tears well up. This was too much for me to take from a suited and booted Bagge, and all when I had invested so much time in feeling concerned about his welfare.

I'm sorry.

I couldn't tell him that I had kept a sleeping watch, that I had witnessed his frightening behaviour during the night.

But you've shaved off all of your hair! I gushed with as much surprise as I could muster.

I fancied a change when I was in town. I often shave it in the summer.

It suits you. Your head is a good shape for it.

He accepted my compliment without a word.

Are you hungry?

No. Thank you.

He turned away and walked up to the house. Curse you, I thought. Nothing more or less than that: curse you. For a moment I imagined that we were married – a challenging state of wedlock; what a frightful prospect it was, me at home and him roaming whenever and wherever he saw fit, like a polar bear, reappearing days later without so much as a word of explanation. A neurosis-inducing, hostile husband. It was hardly surprising his wife had made herself scarce. I was increasingly convinced that she had left him without any intention of returning. Why else would her things be packed away in boxes like they were? It was essentially how I had left my own husband, fleeing without tidying up after myself, leaving him burdened with the task of getting rid of my clothes and belongings after I'd gone, though that was surely nothing compared to facing up to what I had done to him. In the midst of my agitation, Bagge reappeared behind me.

Do you drink gin?

I do drink gin, yes.

He sat down in the garden chair and placed two glasses, two cans of tonic and a bottle on the table. He had changed out of his suit. And there, there it was, the foolish delight had returned, he was bringing out the strong stuff, what in God's name could be better than that?

He handed me a glass and lifted his own in my direction.

Cheers, Allis.

Cheers.

Oh, how good it was. I almost knocked back the first glass in one go; but I forced myself to hold back. I went up to the house and sliced some cucumber, placing it in a small bowl before adding a few ice cubes. Surely there was nothing wrong with making things that little bit more enjoyable.

It was as if he brightened up when he saw me return. I added ice and two slices of cucumber to my glass before topping it up with gin and tonic, as if he might need a practical demonstration, might not know any better. I had a burning desire to speak, but as usual could think of nothing to say. It was possible that he savoured the silence, but he might just as easily find the whole situation exasperating or awkward. Inwardly I pondered how he wanted me to act. I could play any role, it was my greatest talent, fitting in seamlessly regardless of the company I found myself in. I could be anyone for him, if I only had the faintest idea what he wanted.

He topped up his glass, and when he eventually added ice and a slice of cucumber, I felt warm, as if his actions were an endorsement of my character, a mark of his acceptance, part of some kind of policy of approximation.

His bare head was frightfully unfamiliar. Only a millimetre of dark hair remained. Stroking a hand over it would undoubtedly feel lovely, but I missed his dark locks.

As the silence continued, the hurdle to making conversation felt all the more insurmountable. Catching my breath felt almost as impossible, every potential ice-breaker relegated to my internal conversational scrapheap. I had always been that way with everyone, everything that I considered saying aloud first played over and over in my own mind, every utterance a parody of how people in the real world spoke to one another, an optimistic attempt to sound normal, spontaneous. Perhaps there were no troubled waters within him. I felt a fit of giggles rising within me like a rolling wave. I couldn't allow that wave to break. I wanted to sit by his side as his equal. He said nothing, sipping from his small glass. Things would go the same way they always did, beginning with such promise before his mood abruptly faltered and he returned inside. Please, say something, or please, God, let me think of something to say. I felt the laughter building, just as it always did when it shouldn't. Knowing that laughter was the least appropriate thing in any situation was always exactly what initiated it in the first place. It was just another of the many inexplicable, demonic pitfalls laid out for human kind by our bodies and souls, surely designed to ensure our complete and utter humiliation.

I strictly instructed my subconscious to behave, repeating an inner mantra: Pull yourself together. Pull yourself together. Pull yourself together. Bizarrely enough it seemed to work.

Please, help yourself, he said.

Thank you.

I refilled my glass.

It will feel good to get drunk tonight, he announced into thin air. Never before had a statement left me feeling so alive. He had said it, he had announced it; he couldn't break that promise now, couldn't suddenly decide to retire to his bed instead of following through. He would have to stay here for two hours at the very least.

Any special reason?

He sighed. Yes. And no.

Thank you for being so precise, I thought to myself.

Today is a special day.

I didn't ask any more questions. I added a little more gin to my glass, I couldn't taste the alcohol as strongly as I'd like. I hoped it might be viewed by him as a gesture of solidarity.

Suddenly I recalled the stack of debt collection letters I'd received and took a long swig to alleviate the thought. More than anything I wanted to relinquish my responsibilities, even just for the night.

Where were you before you came here? he asked out of the blue.

Where was I? I worked in TV.

You worked in TV? He turned to face me, as if trying to picture it, which was understandable as I also struggled to picture myself as the kind of person who might work in television. And with good reason, I suppose, because I didn't, not anymore.

Yes.

I don't watch much television.

You don't even own a television.

What did you do there?

'There' he had said, as if he were imagining me inside the actual television set.

I presented a programme on Norwegian history.

You were a presenter?

Yes.

On television?

Yes, I snapped, annoyed, was it really that difficult to imagine?

He paused for a moment, then looked at me once again.

But then the series came to end, I suppose.

Well, not exactly.

And you came here.

That's right.

Because you wanted to do something completely different.

Yes.

Because you couldn't be on television anymore.

That's right.

His keen eyes honed in on me.

You had to get away. Far away.

Yes, I had to disappear.

So nobody could get a hold of you.

Absolutely nobody.

He narrowed his eyes.

But why?

What about you, what are you doing out here all on your own like this?

It's your turn.

You're right, I didn't want anyone getting a hold of me. Any more questions?

But why? What could you possibly have done? How long were you on television?

Two years.

Not that long, then. Was it a financial thing?

No, that's one thing it definitely wasn't.

This amused him. I poured us both another drink.

Political? No.

No.

Then that leaves only one possibility.

There are only three possibilities?

You know that as well as I do.

It was like having an animal sitting across from me at the table, a large, long wolf pelt in a garden chair.

Well, it must have been that, then.

Well, well, well, Allis, he said.

He stared into the distance, at the mountains, the pink sky, pondering.

Did you have a...

I turned to face him and our eyes met.

... husband? he asked.

No.

He said no more, draining his glass and closing his eyes. His expression became serious, almost intense, and he was so beautiful that it was painful to observe. I long for him even though he's right here, even though I am sitting just beside him, I thought. He kept his eyes closed, and it struck me all of a sudden that this was how he looked when he made love. With Nor. This was exactly how serious I imagined him looking. I tried to shake the thought, couldn't think such things.

At that very moment he stood up and walked away. He left, as always, without a word, no farewell, goodbye, that's it from me for now.

Bloody, bloody, bloody hell, I thought, downing my glass of unhappiness, of anger. I heard a door open, and moments later he was by my side once again, this time wearing his wool jumper.

I think we both need some flames to gaze into, don't you?

Oh, yes.

He walked down to the bottom of the garden, climbed over the old gate and disappeared down the steps, returning from the jetty carrying the old grill and placing it down before me. I sat quietly, sipping from my glass. He crossed the garden behind me, heading over to the wood stack and returning with an armful of logs before dropping them on the grass. It wasn't long before the flames blazed upwards against the dark night sky and he sat down once again. Fire – is there anything better? There really isn't, I thought to myself.

Are you sure you don't want anything to eat?

What do we have in?

Various bits and pieces, I said.

Don't go to any trouble for my sake.

We've got sausages.

His brow lifted in the way that it rarely ever did, a flicker of hope that all was not lost.

I went inside to fetch the sausages and he hunted down two old, well-worn spit forks, their metal ends burnt black.

We pierced the sausages and rotated the forks slowly, spinning them between our fingers, taking occasional sips of gin.

We ate the sausages straight from the forks. Meat juices dribbled down our chins. I felt elated, a result of the alcohol, of the entire glorious experience. I pierced another sausage with my fork and noticed tiny carvings in the wooden handle, undulating swirls snaking around and around, something carved deep into the wood at the base. N. So they had sat here together, roasting sausages over a fire just like this. That must have been nice. Did she have to come back? She did, of course. But no, she couldn't.

After we finished the sausages, I collected more wood. We both stared into the curling flames, the smoke drifting towards us and stinging our eyes, the birch logs hissing and crackling.

So you're the kind to disappear when things get hard.

I turned to face him. Reclining in his seat, his narrowed eyes didn't give the impression that he cared about having angled such an insult in my direction.

What did you say?

So you'll be leaving here before long, then.

Why, are you planning on making life hard for me?

Perhaps.

I didn't bite. He was doing his best to seem menacing, but he had played that card too many times now.

Good luck with that, I said.

I've been disloyal.

He uttered the words without warning and I grew cold as I gazed at him with surprise. His brow was heavy, it cast a dark shadow over his eyes, his cheekbones and the bridge of his nose highlighted by the moonlight.

Have you?

Yes.

What makes you say that?

He gave no reply.

To whom?

I heard myself slurring my words and straightened up, rousing myself from my relaxed state.

His dark expression, the bare head that I would never get used to.

Everyone.

Everyone on earth?

No.

I saw that he was ready to withdraw into himself once again. I reached out and placed another log on the fire, thinking to myself that for as long as the flames blazed, he would sit by them.

To whom?

He didn't reply. It was midnight, and I was beginning to feel the cold setting in. He seemed to be done with talking for the night. I stood up, the chair creaking beneath me, then went inside to fetch us each a blanket. I hoped that he might be afraid I had gone to bed. To my delight, he wrapped himself in his blanket the moment I handed it to him and we sat there, slightly askew, like two off-balance Indian chiefs, neither of us saying a word.

Do you know what's odd about you? he asked suddenly.

No?

You've never looked me in the eye.

What?

It's true. You don't look me in the eye, you just gaze straight past me.

I do not.

Yes, you do.

I noticed the very same thing about you long ago, I thought, but I said nothing, mostly because it would only sound as if I were copying him.

That's how I knew.

Knew what?

That you'd run away from something.

I said nothing.

He stared straight ahead and breathed deeply.

So you left your job. There aren't as many unknowns in that equation as you might think. You'd probably been given a position that you shouldn't have had in the first place.

I felt sick, drank faster.

And you started at the university, but you didn't go back there after your stint on television.

In a way I was so glad to hear him speak that it overshadowed what he was saying, so I did nothing to stop him.

So you were offered a job that someone else should have had.

He had read the papers, after all, he must know about me. The way he said the words made me feel indignant. He thought he knew it all when really he knew nothing.

I took the job to prevent an utterly unreliable colleague with a fierce political agenda from taking it in my place. That could only have been damaging, it would have been counterfactual historical broadcasting in a prime-time slot, so really, you could say that I did it for ... the Norwegian people.

But how did you get the job in the first place? he asked slowly, gazing into the fire, almost as if he were speaking to himself, like some kind of detective.

You're only asking these questions because you can't imagine me on television, but you should know that I was good at what I did, I cut in abruptly. The programme was moved to Saturday night. And the work involved wasn't easy, you know, it was an extremely demanding role.

I no longer cared that I was slurring my words.

So you got involved with someone who worked there, someone senior to you—

*And* I received an award for my work. Nobody felt it was undeserved. Not until afterwards.

But what came first, him or the job?

He did.

Bad order.

I said nothing.

Did he have to leave too?

I nodded.

Was he very senior?

I nodded again.

How were you found out?

I guarantee that you don't want to know.

I beg to differ.

All right, I thought, if you're so sure. I steeled myself as I fixed my gaze on the flickering flames.

I was invited to their home. It was his wife's fortieth birthday party and the house was full of people. She was so proud to have so many guests that she announced that everyone should leave their coats in the baby's room, and they moved the baby into the box room for the night.

Later on, after the birthday girl had nodded off, he led me into the room where the coats were and we ... well, before we knew it, half the party were hovering in the doorway, gazing on in gleeful disbelief.

But how?

The baby monitor had been left in there even though the baby was sleeping elsewhere.

Gosh.

I said no more. Now he knew.

He leaned his head back and chuckled, rubbing a hand over his face. His laughter was good to hear – the comic potential of the story had increased with the passing of time, I couldn't deny it.

So this was what, February? March?

Yes, a few weeks before I came here.

He turned and looked directly at me.

I won't be away for days at a time from now on.

You won't?

No, that's over now.

I'm not afraid of being here on my own.

But I'm afraid of leaving you on your own.

There are locks on all of the doors.

Even so.

His concern sent a warmth surging through my body.

Do you have enemies locally, then?

A few.

I couldn't tell if it was intended as a joke; it could quite as easily not have been. I started to think about the shopkeeper again, her hushed tones charged with hostility, the woman I had made up my mind to reject, whatever that now meant. I pulled the wool blanket more closely around me. I've started afresh, I thought, I'm doing it. This is it.

Why? What have you done?

He raised his eyebrows.

You don't need to be afraid.

I'm not afraid.

He poured a slug of neat gin into his glass and knocked it back in one go.

If you carry on being this forthcoming then it won't be long before I lose interest in you, I thought. A perpetual human defect, this impulse, enticed by distance and rejection, but as soon as that changes...

What now, then? I asked.

What do you mean?

It's summer. Almost autumn, now.

And?

We didn't really discuss how long you might need me here.

For the summer, he had told me at the start. So I was under the impression that his wife would be back by the autumn. I had let him understand that I was flexible, but I was also careful to imply that I didn't have much to return to when he no longer found that he had much use for me. It wasn't easy to envision what else I could do. He would need help with the fruit picking, but there wasn't much for me to be getting on with after that. There was no work to be done outside in the winter, not beyond a little snow-shovelling at most, and I couldn't really accept payment unless he came up with something else he needed help with around the house.

Do you need me? I asked.

Isn't it you who needs me?

That might be true. But I need to work, if you're going to keep paying me.

What will you do with the money while you're living here?

I have a student loan to pay off.

There are always odd jobs that need doing around the house. It's more than a hundred years old, you know.

Is it?

Yes, built in 1890.

What you really need is some kind of historic property expert, not me.

It's getting late, he said.

Not that late.

I threw another log on the fire to keep him where he was.

I'll need some wood for the winter too, Allis.

No longer us, just him. How quickly things changed.

But this evening has been so nice.

A person can stay outside for as long as they like if they just make up their mind to do so, he said, as if it were some kind of enigmatic proclamation of truth.

Having offered too much of himself he was now forced to turn back to being difficult. It was too predictable. He acted like a puppet master, and I needed to become better at asserting my independence rather than being endlessly controlled by his whims. The light of the flames flickered across his face, illuminating the lines and creases, and this image of him evoked criminality of some kind or another; he exuded punishment. Once his hair had grown back, even just a little, it would be thick and dark, infinitely handsome. He was clean-shaven for the first time since I had known him, but I only noticed it now, his cheeks smooth, a cleft in his chin that I hadn't previously observed. He looked more dangerous. I reached out for another log, couldn't bear the thought of him going anywhere.

Ow!

I held my hand up to the light of the fire to find a splinter plunged deep into the flesh of my index finger.

What is it?

A splinter.

I pressed at it with my fingertips, but only succeeded in embedding it more deeply.

Let me see.

I stood up to make my way towards the light. He followed me.

Let me see.

I stopped and held out my hand under the outside light on the veranda.

It's nothing, it's only tiny.

I'll get it for you.

You're drunk, you'll only make things worse.

Nonsense.

He walked through the veranda door and I followed him, taking a seat at the table. He re-appeared from his bedroom moments later with a needle pinched between his fingertips.

Is it a sewing room you've got in there?

He laughed.

Don't you want to use tweezers?

It's better with a needle. Trust me.

I looked at him and felt my insides turn to ice. He lit the candle on the chest of drawers and held the needle up to the flame. A red glow flickered across his face. He pulled the needle from the heat and looked at me.

Do you want a swig of gin first?

Yes.

He went outside and returned with the bottle, passing it to me. He held the needle to the flame once again as I took a mouthful, as if it would make the slightest difference now. He sat down in the chair opposite me, grasped my hand and looked straight at me, his expression mild but firm.

It's important that you stay very still.

I'm not sure this is a good idea.

Very still.

OK.

I thought about how much he had had to drink then looked the other way.

Allis, he whispered softly. There's something I need to tell you.

What is it?

Something I've been thinking about lately.

I heard him swallow.

What?

He said nothing.

What were you going to say?

Gotcha. He held the splinter triumphantly up to the light.

Surprised, I gazed up at it and then down again at my hand, still held in his. He let go.

Wait here.

He stood up and made his way to the bathroom, fetching some antiseptic ointment and cotton wool. He sat down and took my hand once again.

This'll be fine. It's not bleeding.

Thank you.

How does it feel?

You were about to say something, I thought to myself.

Fine.

He didn't let go of my hand. As we sat there together, I thought: it's about time, now. It's about time. Let me in.

Time for bed, I think. He let go of my hand and stood up. Goodnight, Allis.

Goodnight.

I sank. Motionless, I remained there until he was inside his bathroom. Bagge, Bagge. Please, tread softly on my heart. I traipsed up the stairs. This wasn't on. I brushed my teeth, washed my face and went to bed, my heart stuttering in my chest, fast-paced, knowing the amount I'd had to drink would never allow me to fall asleep. I heard him emerge once again from his bathroom. I closed my eyes. Don't you understand anything at all?

*

I awoke with a sense of unease. In the middle of a dream I had remembered the fire we'd left burning outside. It was unlikely, but the past few days had been so dry, if an ember were to fly up and drift away ... I got up out of bed and walked over to the window. The fire was out, but there, beside what was left of it sat Bagge, stock-still in his chair. The sight of him was like a knife to the heart. Not because he wanted to be alone, but because of the way he had gone about it. There he sat, by himself in the darkness, mining the depths of his own soul. I didn't like it. It was three o'clock in the morning. What can you possibly be mulling over like this? Without warning, he turned his head and looked straight at me. Without thinking I stepped aside, away from the window, but there could be no doubt-ing that he'd seen me. I stood by the wall, rigid, motionless. I only got up to check the fire! Should I call down to him, tell him that? Shout out of the window? I didn't need to shout the words, even if I were to whisper them I knew that he'd still hear me, it was as silent as the grave out there.

I went back to my bed, my heart beating all the faster, pulling the sheets up and over my head. But enclosed in the darkness, everything felt all the more overwhelming.

I heard his footsteps on the stairs. Fast-paced, heavy, straight to my door. He's going to kill me. He's coming to finish me off. I don't know why the thought leapt into my mind.

Allis.

He was standing outside my door, his voice thick, strange.

I only got up to check the fire was out!

Silence.

Can you come out here?

What is it?

He said nothing else, but I heard his breathing through the door.

Answer me! I insisted, close to wailing.

Can I come in?

What do you want?

There was a key in the door on my side, I could bound across the room and turn it, lock him out, but still I lay there, paralysed.

What do you want?

Let me in!

No! I whimpered.

He fell silent, then I heard the sound of his heavy breathing once again. My heart hammered in my chest, my eyes never once leaving the door. I couldn't move.

My God, he moaned softly. I'm sorry.

I held my breath, lying completely still.

I'm sorry.

What is it? My voice was at breaking point.

I didn't realise that I was frightening you. I'm sorry.

I didn't answer him.

I'm sorry, Allis. I didn't mean to scare you.

I said nothing.

Do you want to go to sleep? Can I come in for a bit?

It's unlocked.

The door opened slowly. He stood before me, gazing at me with his deep, dark eyes; he must have had much more to drink since I turned in for the night. Confused, he took an unsteady step into the room before sinking down onto his knees.

I'm sorry, Allis.

It's alright.

He threw one arm behind him and closed the door.

You're blind drunk.

He looked up.

There's a hammer on your bedside table.

I need to be able to defend myself.

Can I sleep on your floor, Allis?

On my floor?

He didn't reply.

I placed a pillow on the floor, on top of the rug.

I don't have an extra cover, I told him.

I'm sorry... he slurred, flipping over onto his side.

He closed his eyes and instantly drifted off into a deep sleep. Slowly I shook my head. A child. His back rose and fell as he lay there, his bare head resting on one arm. What was he? These sudden eruptions, the wolf in him. All the same, I felt so warm and safe having him there, curled up on my bedroom floor. I closed my eyes and turned to face the wall.

Two hours later I was forced to wake him. It had started with whimpering and shallow breathing, his knuckles white, his body tensed, his shoulder blades digging into the floor. Then he had started howling. I reached a hand down and gently shook him by the shoulder.

You're dreaming.

His eyes shot open and he gasped for air.

No!

Yes. You're dreaming.

He looked at me, then sank back and closed his eyes once again.

My God.

What were you dreaming about?

He buried his face into the pillow, saying nothing.

What was it?

I could tell from the sound of his breathing that he was fast asleep once again.

When I awoke, he was gone. The pillow had been left on the floor, but other than that there was no trace of him.

He was sitting at the table when I arrived downstairs. Inwardly I hoped that he wouldn't feel embarrassed, forced to compensate by treating me with his traditional icy contempt. But he wasn't angry. He looked up at me and smiled.

Good morning.

Good morning, I replied. I felt a warmth surge through my body from deep within.

There won't be any repeats of last night. I must have been very drunk.

It's fine. It was nice to have a visitor.

I didn't know where I was when I woke up, he said, smiling self-consciously.

I put the coffee on and set the table. He ate voraciously and was quick to laugh, talkative. Perhaps he was still drunk. I stood at the kitchen worktop, coffee cup in hand, a presence he didn't seem to find invasive. If either of us was being invasive, it was him. After he had finished his breakfast, I felt compelled to ask him.

Do you remember what you dreamt about last night?

Last night?

You had a nightmare. Don't you remember? I had to wake you.

You woke me up?

You fell asleep again straight away.

He looked as if he were considering things for a moment.

It must have been awful. You were covered in sweat. You were screaming.

Screaming? What was I screaming?

Well, more like howling, really.

He chuckled briefly.

You must have been terrified. Did I say anything?

Nothing that I could make out.

I don't remember a thing.

After he spoke, he fell silent. He looked as if he were gathering his thoughts about the forgotten episode. I stood up and cleared the table, pouring the last of the coffee into his cup. As I washed the dishes, he turned his chair around to face me.

What is it?

I just remembered.

Remembered?

I've never told you about the time that I was taken, he said, looking at me.

Taken?

Yes. Perhaps you should know.

I turned to him.

What do you mean, taken?

Well, I still don't know for certain who they were. They came in the middle of the night and seized me. Five or six of them, big men. Nor was here with me, but they tore her from my arms and bundled me into the back of a van.

What?

I sat down at the table.

We drove for hours. I lay on the floor in the back, tied up, slamming against the walls of the van whenever they turned a corner. I heard barking. Then the van stopped, we had arrived, the back doors were opened and they pulled me out. We were at the edge of a coniferous forest. It was the middle of winter, there was snow all around, the branches of the trees were weighed down by it. We marched into the forest, each of them shoving me deeper and deeper in. Nobody said a word. I couldn't see their faces, they were all wearing balaclavas, dark clothing, boots, I remember thinking they must be ex-military. There wasn't a sound, only our breathing and the occasional whimper from the dogs. There were two or three of them ahead of me, and just as many behind. I knew that I couldn't get away. After a while I realised that we were getting close – the dogs started barking, on and on and on, then howling. By the time we reached a clearing in the forest they were wild, leaping up and down, straining at their chains, the men shaking their fists and beating the dogs' snouts to silence them. They drew back into the snow and whimpered quietly.

Bagge said no more, returning home, as I had begun to think of it when he so often and so abruptly fell silent and grew distant.

And? What then?

He looked up at me inquisitively.

What else?

They gave me a chair.

A chair.

Someone behind me brought out a chair. We were standing in the middle of the clearing, and I was allowed to sit down. I sat there, my hands still tied behind my back, cold, my head bare. I was dead beat after the trek through the forest.

I was perched on the edge of my seat, cold with shock and anguish at the tale that was unfolding.

Then the men that had taken me brought several more chairs out, lining them up in two rows in the snow in front of me. The chair in the centre was much larger than the others. Men and women appeared, emerging from the woodland on all sides. They all wore long, dark cloaks and masks, bird masks that covered their faces. There were twelve of them, birds of every species, a raven and a magpie, a gull and a great tit and a robin. I saw a swan. A buzzard. One woman wore a mask that covered her whole head, a mallard. It was an incredible sight, astonishingly beautiful, shimmering green on top of the body of a woman dressed in dark garments. I did nothing but stare at her.

I started to laugh, and he looked up at me, startled.

You're pulling my leg, aren't you?

I'm not!

I looked at him, puzzled.

I realised then that this was a tribunal. My case was to be heard. The twelve judges sat in silence and stared straight ahead from behind their bird masks. My guards stood in a straight line behind me, and I turned around to find that they had removed their balaclavas: one had the head of a halibut, blind on one side with two eyes on the other. One had the head of a toad. One had the head of a mouse. One had the shining black head of an adder. I felt an intense, pulsating rush in my ears, but when the head judge stepped forward, I did all that I could to look her in the eye and hold her gaze. She wore an eagle mask. She instructed me to stand. She read my name aloud and announced that I was charged with *skemdarvig*. I wasn't familiar with the term, but still I knew what she meant. She asked whether I pleaded guilty. I shook my head. We saw you, one of the judges cried, and my eyes scanned the rows and landed on the gull, I knew it was she who had called out. I shook my head yet again. The judges turned to one another and whispered, conferring. I stood bolt upright, my back straight. After that, things moved quickly. The judge in the eagle mask read the verdict: it had been prepared and written down beforehand; I was given no chance to make a statement of my own. She sentenced me to death. 'The nature of your evil deeds make you nothing but a foul *nithing*.' As she said the words, I looked again at the mallard and she turned away from me. It was only then that I recognised her: it was Nor.

I sat there, unflinching, listening to every word he said.

And then you woke me up.

So it *was* a dream! Bloody hell, Sigurd! You told me it wasn't!

What?

You were talking about it as if it had actually happened!

That was what I dreamt about last night... he replied, confused.

I was sitting here listening as if this had actually happened to you, as if you had actually been dragged out into the forest, it was awful.

He laughed with surprise.

Well, it was a very lucid dream.

I shook my head, then rinsed and squeezed out a cloth, wiping the table in front of him. Deep in thought he sat there, gazing vacantly into the air in front of him, paying no heed to me as I carried on around him. He rubbed a hand over his stubble. Fortunately his hair had started to grow back more noticeably, even just overnight. A thick, dark layer. When I turned on the tap he was wrenched from his thoughts, pushing his chair back from the table and hastily thanking me for breakfast.

I pulled the dictionaries from the living room shelf and carried them up to my room after he left me. I had come across the word before, but I couldn't find it listed in any of the books. I tried some alternative spellings and eventually found *skjemtarverk*, used to describe an irremediable act, a crime so serious that no fine or any other kind of reparation could atone for it. It was listed in an old copy of the national law of King Magnus the Law-Mender, 'Magnus Lagabøtes landslov'. The culprit was proclaimed an outlaw and any man was free to take his life. *Skjemtarverk* described the vilest of human behaviour, I read, murder, mutilation, the height of dishonourable actions. A *nithing* was the most contemptible of life forms, a person whose honour had been entirely removed. What did it mean, dreaming of this kind of thing? It's hardly as if I was totally unfamiliar with the irrational reasoning of dreams: I was capable of imagining that I was anything from a prisoner of war to an executioner, regardless of the time of day. But the degree of precision in his story, the logical chronology, so certain, so animated. Not like any other dream, where everything seems to be perfectly in order as you lie there, but which swiftly disintegrates in the light of day, leaving behind nothing but flaky fragments of some back-to-front world. The fact that his wife had been in the dream, and all as he had been lying on my bedroom floor. The glistening green mallard's head. A rapture of guilt.

I was careful to buy everything we needed to avoid having to return to the shop later in the week. Eventually I placed the basket on the counter. Just keep your head down and your mouth shut, I thought, my dislike palpable in every nerve ending. She said nothing, I did the same, and she began entering my items into the register. The red, nubbly skin of her throat, just beneath her weak chin. After I handed her the money, she stopped for a moment.

Yes, that was a terrible business with his wife.

What?

I looked at her and held her gaze to show my strength. I couldn't let her think she could get away with slinging malicious comments around for me to drag home like some kind of idiot.

Not that there was any way out.

I'm sorry, I'm not sure I know what you—

Perhaps you weren't invited to the funeral? Too much to be getting on with in the 'garden', eh?

A smirk flickered across her lips as she handed me my change.

I left without a word, opening my bicycle panniers and shoving the things I'd bought inside so aggressively that I felt eggs breaking. I had to tell Bagge, he had to know what she had said. Not a single neighbouring house anywhere near his, and yet she knew that I worked in the garden. That was the stupidest part, the thing that agitated me most was the idea of someone observing my pathetic attempts at gardening. The image of him, clean-shaven, standing there in his black suit. Was that how things really were? I couldn't allow the woman in the shop to gain any more control over me than she already had. As long as I thought of her as no more than a shopkeeper – not as an individual, but as part of some vague, hostile force – then it would be easier to kill her, I thought. But she already had a face, a voice. Could it really be true that his wife was dead? 'Not that there was any way out'.

\*

He didn't come out of his room when dinner was ready. I knocked at his door several times, called out from the veranda. He was gone. I slipped my feet into my sandals and made my way down through the garden. I found him at the end of the jetty in a light shirt, fishing rod in hand.

So this is where you're hiding. Dinner is ready.

He turned around.

Damn it, I'd forgotten all about the time.

Caught anything?

Nothing.

He followed me up the steps.

Aren't you having anything? he asked, as I placed the plate on the table before him.

You usually eat alone.

Do I?

My God, yes, you have done ever since I arrived. I always eat after you.

Why is that?

Because you told me that's the way it would be. I eat after you've gone back into your room.

He gazed up at me in disbelief. He seemed to be struggling to believe it. I almost asked him if he had gone mad, but I didn't dare say the words aloud in case there were some truth in them.

But doesn't your food get cold?

I nodded in the direction of the stove.

That's why I use the foil.

But don't you want to eat with me, I mean, wouldn't that be simpler?

Well, yes. Is that what you want?

Of course I do, Allis.

I set a place directly opposite him. This is it, I thought, she was right, I'm forcing my way in. She would always be right.

It was the first time we had eaten together, indoors in any case; we'd cooked the fish and sausages outside, but this was a formal situation, an institution, dinner at the table. The man sitting opposite me, I thought, is this a man in mourning? Yes, of course, that's it, he's in shock. Confusion and memory loss, textbook symptoms. Could it be true? Where had she been all this time, had it been a long, drawn-out illness? He'd hardly left the house since I'd been here, he had only taken, what, four trips into town since April?

This is good. What is it?

It's coley.

From the shop?

I nodded.

We ate in silence. I did what I could to prevent my cutlery from clinking against the crockery, avoided alerting him to my presence in case he had forgotten that I was there. He chewed his fish slowly, his knife and fork tiny in his huge hands, taking the occasional sip of his water. His hair was sleek and black, thick stubble covering his chin, he hadn't shaved since he had come home. I had no idea how to ask him, I wanted to get it out of the way before we finished eating, but the food on his plate gradually disappeared and I found myself unable to say a word.

Eventually he stood up.

Thank you for that.

You're welcome.

I had to say something. I took a deep breath.

Sigurd.

He turned.

Yes?

Would you like a cup of coffee?

Yes, please. Maybe in half an hour or so?

OK, half an hour it is.

I sighed inwardly, wondering if there was a number you could call, some kind of national or municipal authority you could contact to find out if somebody had died. No, I couldn't bring myself to do it. But the newspaper, the obituaries. If the funeral had taken place on Friday, then it was possible there was an announcement on Monday or

Tuesday or sometime thereabouts. But no. I cast the thought aside once again, this wasn't something that I should be getting involved with.

When we were sitting at the table with our coffee, I made the mistake of bringing up what I'd been mulling over.

The woman in the shop, I heard myself mutter into the air absent-mindedly.

Yes?

Do you know her well?

He looked at me, puzzled.

Do I know the woman in the shop well? No, not at all.

No? OK.

Why?

How should I put it? I tried to recall the exact words she had used, then took a deep breath.

She's been making comments recently.

His grey eyes locked onto my own.

What kind of comments?

I tried to remember her exact words.

It all started – I swallowed – when I had to stick my name under yours on the letter box, because—

What did you say?

He placed his cup down on the table beside the saucer.

Because my mother had received a batch of post for me, and she needed to forward it to me.

You put your name on my letter box? When?

When you were away, last week.

He said nothing.

It was only there for a day. Two at the most.

What kind of comments has she been making?

Just odd things.

Like what?

It's as if she wants to isolate me, to try to frighten me.

What has she been saying?

I took a deep breath.

Is your wife dead?

He stood up.

You can't go.

He remained there as if his feet were pinned to the floor.

Sigurd, please—

Yes, she is.

He stood there, staring at me intently as he uttered the words.

Yes, she's dead.

I felt something inside me fall away as he said the words, while another part of me seemed to soar.

Did it happen long ago?

I tried to utter the words as tenderly as possible.

When I was away.

He didn't look at me, his gaze transfixed on something and nothing in thin air before him. I didn't want to say too much, I wanted to let him decide if he wanted to talk about it or not.

I'm so sorry.

He took a seat once again, sideways this time, facing away from me.

Thank you. Did she say anything else, the woman in the shop?

No, nothing in particular.

He gazed vacantly straight ahead.

Was she ill?

Yes, what else?

He was so hostile that I didn't dare ask any more questions. I remained where I was, not touching my coffee for fear that it might seem that I lacked respect. I wanted to say 'I feel for you', but it would have sounded ridiculous. He gave no indication that he might say anything else, but he remained where he was.

Was it the funeral you came home from on Friday?

Yes.

He had acted so strangely that day, the way he had slept on my bedroom floor that night, and yet at the same time he had never been better company.

I'm so sorry.

You've nothing to apologise for.

No, no. So he wasn't interested in platitudes. It was fine, I could understand that. But why hadn't there been any other signs? Had she fallen ill on this trip of hers, or was that just another fabrication? All of her things in the locked room upstairs, it must have been a long time since she had last lived here. We sat there for a good, long while, neither of us saying a word. I was glad he didn't get up and leave me.

Can I get you anything?

He looked up.

There's some coffee left.

Yes. Thanks.

I stood up to pour it into his cup. All of a sudden he grasped my wrist and the glass pot fell to the floor and shattered, coffee spilling everywhere. He held me tightly, roughly, then hissed at me.

It's just question after question with you, you never stop!

I'm sorry!

He let me go and I fell back, took a few steps away from him, managed to regain my balance, then heard the crunch of glass beneath my feet. Fortunately I was wearing slippers. *Her* slippers. He leapt up and stormed out and into his room. I could hear my pulse thumping in my ears, everything had happened so quickly.

The dustpan and brush were stacked up by the fridge, and I managed to sweep up the shards of glass on the floor, hunched over all the while, head bowed, convinced he was skulking behind me, constantly prepared to duck out of the way. I ran a cloth under the tap, got down on my hands and knees and mopped up the spilt coffee, then, hearing his bedroom door open, I glanced over my shoulder.

Allis, I'm sorry.

How many times would he have to say it?

It's OK.

I mean it, I'm so sorry about what happened.

And I mean it, it's OK.

I stood up, walked over to the kitchen worktop without looking at him and rinsed out the cloth.

You have to forgive me.

I turned around.

I do! I forgive you! I forgive you whatever it is that needs forgiving!

He looked at me, aggrieved. I took a step towards him.

It really doesn't matter, I mean it. Here.

I reached out a hand and he took it, squeezed it tightly in his own, his eyes closed. He pulled me close in an embrace with his free arm, my nose pressed up against the hollow of his throat, my arms hanging limp by my sides, I could hear his heart beating. He let go of my hand and wrapped both of his arms around me, squeezing me tight. My knees trembled. He grasped my shoulders and gently pushed me away, gripping me with both hands, staring at me with a grave expression.

Allis.

He let me go. I was on the verge of collapsing, like a ragdoll. I grasped the dustpan and opened the kitchen cupboard, tipping the shards of glass into the dustbin and hearing them clink against one another as they landed.

Allis.

I looked up.

You need to get away from me.

What?

He stood up straight and looked down at me, then swiftly shook his head.

No, he said. I'm sorry.

I didn't know what to do or say. I bent down to pick up a stray piece of glass from beneath the table, where it glittered in the evening light. He just stood there, observing me with a sorrowful expression. Now is the time to be generous, I thought. My God, the man has only just buried his wife. He turned away from me and headed back to his room.

Instead of crying I drew in deep breaths, I had nothing to cry about, though I had once read that, chemically, tears had a soothing effect. I felt the pressure of my subdued sobs fill my chest as I stood up and started on the washing up.

Just as I finished up, he re-emerged.

Allis, can you come outside with me?

I turned around, surprised, slightly afraid.

Now?

There's something I need to show you.

What is it?

He put on a pair of shoes that had been left by the veranda and opened the door.

You'll see. Fetch a jumper.

Slowly I walked towards him, slipping my feet into my sandals and following him through the garden into the red, warm June evening. He headed in the direction of the steps leading down to the jetty.

You know I don't swim.

I know.

I followed him down the steps. Darkness was beginning to fall. I was afraid of him, he was unstable, he could be about to show me any-thing; I pictured his wife's coffin in the boathouse, all manner of ideas charging through my mind as I made my way down the steps. He must have sensed it, because he stopped and turned to face me.

There's nothing to be afraid of.

That's exactly what he would have said even if there *were* something to fear, I thought.

When we reached the jetty, the garden chairs were already down there waiting for us.

Sit down.

He passed me a blanket.

Was this what he wanted to show me, the fact that he had carried the garden furniture down here? For a long while we sat without speaking, gazing out over the water as the sun set, a mild evening breeze blowing in, everything otherwise still and tranquil.

By around nine o'clock I was beginning to grow impatient.

What was it that you wanted to show me?

Wait.

All right, then.

All kinds of thoughts ran through my mind as I sat there, slightly drowsy, slightly cold. I thought about my life before: university, television, cities I'd visited, childhood summer holidays, conversations I'd had with people I barely even knew but which I still remembered word for word to that day, bicycle rides and the supermarket where I used to do my shopping when I first moved away from home, my grandmother's handwriting.

There, he said.

What?

Look, now.

What?

The moon.

The moon had suddenly taken on a deep-red hue, a searing white crescent around the top half of the glowing sphere.

A lunar eclipse, I said.

Yes.

I've never understood how they work.

Well, what if you had to make a guess?

I'd much rather not.

Come on, you're not getting out of this one.

I was being called upon to reveal my true ignorance. A solar eclipse was fair enough, but what about this?

Uhm, the sun passes between the earth and the moon?

He shook his head with the merest flash of a smile.

I thought hard.

No, OK. Well, I don't know.

The earth passes between the sun and the moon. The moon is in the earth's shadow.

So there's no sunlight on the moon's surface?

Exactly.

I regretted not having thought things through more thoroughly.

The shadow cast on the moon, it's the earth's shadow?

The earth's shadow, sweeping over the surface of the moon. For a moment there was something so powerful in that. It was like seeing the earth from a new perspective, even if only in the form of a shadow, and a tiny fraction of one at that.

It was how Aristotle proved that the earth is round, he said.

Ever so slowly, the moon was consumed by the red gloom. We sat in silence and observed the spectacle taking place before us.

Right about now, he said, that's it at its smallest.

We sat there in almost complete darkness and silence, not a sound beyond the gentle lapping of the water and his breathing, only just loud enough to be heard. I felt content, calm. And unhappy. I had a strong desire to speak freely, properly, seriously, but it was impossible. Perhaps he wanted the same thing, but he had to be the one to go first. I wanted to hear about his wife. Had they been living apart? Why? I was sitting beside a widower.

Let me look at you.

What?

Let me look at you, he repeated.

I turned to face him.

You're beautiful, Allis.

Now that it's dark, maybe.

Beautiful in the light, too.

Do you really think so?

Yes. Of course.

You're a handsome man.

I'd said it now. But he had been the one to say it first. My face grew warm; I couldn't help but smile. He got up, standing in front of me as the deep-red orb disappeared behind him.

Let me look at you.

I sat and stared up at him, smiling warily.

Let me see.

I gazed up at him, puzzled, unsure what it was that he wanted from me.

You're so beautiful.

Thank you.

Don't you want to take off that big coat, Allis?

This was it. But here? With some hesitation I pulled my arms out of the coat sleeves and laid it across my lap, sitting there in nothing but my flimsy t-shirt. He sighed, his mouth slightly open, his tongue pressing against his front teeth.

So beautiful.

I parted my lips slightly and looked up at him.

My darling. Darling Allis.

I didn't know what to say.

You have to let me see you. More of you. Can I, please?

Could he? He stood over me, the moonlight forging a faint contour all around him. His gaze was mild and dark, tender. Slowly I pulled my t-shirt over my head.

Oh, Allis.

He sighed again.

You have to show me.

It was cold. I felt goose bumps rising in the cool night air. I looked up at him, uncertain. He gave an almost imperceptible nod. I reached around behind my back with both hands and unhooked my bra, taking it off and placing it on the wall. His eyes narrowed.

Oh, Allis, he whispered.

I trembled slightly. Breathed deeply. He took a step forward and leaned down towards me. Gently, he pressed his face to my cheek, his lips to my ear. I closed my eyes, his warm breath sending chills down my spine.

Whore.

He stood up and turned to face the fjord, the moon, then slowly climbed the steps up towards the house.

I felt a prickling sensation behind my eyes, every sound distant, muffled. I was aware only of my own breath, every gasp for air stinging my lungs. My legs quickly lost their strength, but I had to keep going. Only black mountains, grey fields and dark windows, scarcer with every passing mile. Only an expanding nothingness lay before me. Like cycling out of the cosmos. The roomy work jacket kept the upper half of me warm, but my hands and feet were ice-cold, clad in nothing but lightweight sandals. How could a main road be so deserted? I would need to stop and rest before long, but there was hardly a bus stop along the way, only the roadside ditch and a guard rail separating me from the sheer cliff-side that dropped down to the fjord, the water glittering with self-satisfaction in the moonlight. I had no plan, only knew I couldn't stop, couldn't turn back, not this time, I had to get away.

I had set off in the opposite direction from the shop, which was also the opposite direction to the town, as well as to my parents. I couldn't be certain how far I was from the nearest village, for all I knew I might be stumbled upon the following morning at a quayside somewhere, frozen to death down by the fjord.

Just as I was considering turning around, I started to see houses appearing along the way. The road became wider, a yellow line appearing in the middle, just around a bend, I must be getting close to something. My legs were stiff and numb, my toes blue-white in their sandals. My last ounce of strength helped me up a gentle incline, my feet pedalling laboriously. When I reached the crest of the hill, I stopped and looked out over the horizon, the bright light of the sign down below. I was too weary to feel happiness, but made a mental note and freewheeled downhill. I hopped off my bicycle and my knees almost gave way beneath me, forcing me to lean against one of the petrol pumps for support. I pushed the bicycle around the corner in the dark of the night. The automatic doors slid open. A woman in a red uniform with brown hair pulled back in a ponytail glanced up from behind the counter with a look of surprise.

Could I use the toilet, please?

She looked me up and down quickly before nodding in the direction of the door. Aching and stiff, my teeth chattered as I made my way there. Once inside, I closed the door behind me and turned on the hot tap. I held my hands beneath the searing hot water and watched them turn from white to dark pink, swelling under the running water. I splashed some water on my face and rubbed away the sweat and dust from the road. I ran a hand through my hair, brushing it from my face and scraping it into a ponytail with a hair tie I found in the pocket of my shorts. I straightened up, pulled my shoulders back and inhaled deeply, shaking, a crackling in my ears, the taste of blood in my mouth, still out of breath. My hands trembled from gripping the bicycle handlebars so tightly. The fluorescent light on the ceiling blinked, a cleaning schedule hanging by the mirror on the wall. A ballpoint pen dangled from a piece of string. People's signatures, each one a statement: Yes, I was here, I cleaned this toilet on this date or that date. Everything in order. It suddenly struck me as so significant, every signature symbolic of a clean, industrial bleach and rubber gloves. I felt tears welling up. Civilisation. The sight of myself in his enormous dark-blue coat, hastily unhooked from where it had been left hanging by the woodpile. How insignificant I was, in spite of everything. I could so easily lose my grip; I could so easily be crushed by almost anything. My endurance threshold was so very low. Whenever anything became difficult, I realised just how little I was capable of withstanding, how pathetically weak my backbone truly was, followed by a quivering lower lip and an imminent escape.

A brief knock at the door, timid.

I need to close up now.

I'm coming, I replied hurriedly. Turned the tap on again, stuck my hands under the stream, turned it off again, dried them with a paper towel. Unlocked the door. She was standing by the exit with a bunch of keys in one hand.

Is everything alright? she asked, looking down at my feet, my toes bare, my shorts just visible under the bulky work jacket. She cast a glance outside.

You didn't drive here?

I cycled.

You're not wearing much. Are you going far?

I hesitated.

Can I drive you anywhere?

I looked at her. Ten years older than me, maybe. The kind of wonderfully dependable person that this country is filled with, efficient and kind, a mother to all in need. Brown hair and freckles, resolute, with a wide stance, just the kind of person you could depend upon to help sort things out when required. In that instant I realised I had become the kind of person that needed help, the care of others. I was filled with a leaden depression at the thought of being so isolated. While others were of flesh and blood, eating together, weeping together, I was a scarecrow out in the field, human-like yet not quite human, cut off from society, all alone; but a scarecrow at least had a purpose, and that was something that I lacked.

I'll make space for your bicycle in the back.

I walked towards her, looking outside. There was a motel just over the road. I could stay there for the night, explain the money situation, ask to have the invoice forwarded onto me. How far was it to the airport from here? There would probably be buses passing through here on the hour, or I could take a taxi there, assure the driver that I'd pay him as soon as I was able to. And the plane ticket? That kind of thing sorted itself out, anyone could see that I wasn't in a great place in life, and isn't that what people do? Help each other out when it's needed most? I could take the plane back to Johs, we could try again. It wasn't a crazy idea, and perhaps the time was right.

Feeling somewhat uplifted, I realised that this was my greatest strength: I was a problem-solver, in spite of everything, forever forward planning when I found myself in a sticky situation, immediately preparing my potential escape routes, and always with a trace of enthusiasm, because difficult circumstances were good starting points for life changes, great or small. That was exactly how it had been with K: I'd been struck by the sudden realisation that I could finally withdraw from society with good reason. That had been how I had stumbled across the advertisement.

She stood there, waiting for me to answer. She looked like a referee for a handball team in her red uniform.

Which way are you headed?

North, she replied.

Me too.

Great! Let's go, she said, holding the door open for me before turning out the lights and locking up after us. I fetched the bicycle from around the corner, wheeling it over to her pickup truck and lifting it up and into the back. I took a seat in the front, she started the car and we drove away from the petrol station.

Are you going far? she asked.

Not far.

Do you have somewhere to sleep tonight?

Yes.

Slowly I trundled the bicycle along the drive, leaves crackling under the wheels as I passed between the pale trunks of the birch trees, the picket fence and house before me. There was no sign of light in any of the windows. I leaned my bicycle up against the fence, silently opened and closed the gate and approached the house as quietly as possible. I was determined, I could feel it pulsing through my body, filling every blood cell. I wasn't going to turn around. I made my way along the outer walls of the house and up the steps, my sandals clacking, then pushed smoothly and silently on the door handle. Locked. I walked back down the steps, a cacophony of thoughts and voices crowding my mind. I stepped off to one side of the flagstones as I walked around the house, climbed the two steps leading up onto the veranda and walked up to the veranda door, attempting to look through the glass into the darkness of the living room. My gaze roamed around the room, from the kitchen at the far end to the tiny stove, the table, his chair – I found myself staring at a pale face, two large eyes glaring back at me. I screamed, clutched at my heart and screamed straight at him. He was motionless in his chair, a dead gaze. I stumbled backwards and was on the brink of losing my balance when I saw him leap from where he had been sitting and tear open the veranda doors.

Go away!

His eyes were dark hollows, he looked ill, as if he were soon to depart this world.

No! I cried back at him, clenching my jaw, teetering on the edge of the veranda, every muscle in my body tensed. You need me!

No, Allis! You need to get away from me!

I paused, then grabbed at one of the herb pots hanging along the veranda railing and threw it down at our feet. Shards of terracotta and earth flew upwards. He shrank back.

No! I'm not going anywhere. You're in mourning.

He looked down calmly, slowly shaking his head.

No. I'm not.

Don't you get it? I asked.

He looked up at me. The cold and distress was making me shake, my feet bare but for my sandals, my long, cold legs protruding from my shorts and his coat. My teeth chattered, a sudden and overwhelming power flowing through me from the indignation deep within my chest.

I have nowhere else to go!

I shuddered, his image hazy, stepped to one side and then back, darkness consuming me, dizziness coursing through me, watching as he lurched in my direction.

Sounds from the kitchen downstairs woke me. Intense delight radiated through me, I was here. My body was damp with sweat, the sheets clinging to me. I tried sitting up in bed but my arms couldn't take the weight. The noises I'd heard from downstairs came to a halt. I heard his footsteps on the stairs.

Allis? he murmured outside my bedroom door, knocking softly. His close-cropped head peered around the door.

How are you?

How did I get up here?

I carried you up last night.

Is it early?

It's morning. Can I get you anything?

Something for my fever. Have a look in the bathroom cabinet.

He left the room and returned with two tablets that he placed in the palm of my hand, followed by a glass of water. I swallowed the tablets and lay back down. He left the room, the sound of his steps on the staircase followed by rustling in the kitchen. After a short while I heard him returning upstairs. He knocked on the door and came in carrying a glass of red juice and a steaming bowl.

Porridge.

He set it down on my bedside table with a hint of pride. I smiled weakly and thanked him. He left. I laid my head back on my pillow, couldn't face the prospect of eating anything in spite of his pride. I closed my eyes, a cold shiver creeping over me. I flipped onto my side and waited for the tablets to take effect. My skin felt paper-thin, so delicate.

When I woke up again he was sitting at my desk and looking at me. The bowl remained untouched on the bedside table.

What's the time?

Almost four.

In the morning?

He chuckled silently, shaking his head. He leaned in towards me, calmly placing a hand on my forehead.

We need to take your temperature, he said, picking up a thermometer from the desk and carefully placing it between my lips. It bleeped after a few moments and he snatched it out and reviewed it, his forehead wrinkled.

Get some sleep, Allis.

When I next woke up, I was alone. The light outside told me it was early evening, and I was trembling, my muscles aching. I listened for noises from downstairs, but heard nothing. After a while I heard a bicycle creaking as it was wheeled through the garden, then his footsteps, outside, up the stairs, at the door. I closed my eyes and turned to face the wall. From the other side of the door I heard a knock, I didn't answer. He gently pushed the door open and stepped inside. For a moment he stood silent and motionless in the middle of the room, then I heard him remove something from a bag and place it on the bedside table. He retraced his steps out of the room and left the door ajar, I regretted having pretended to be asleep. I turned to look; he had left me a bag of grapes.

I'd had nightmares, but I couldn't recall what they had been about, only felt aware of the night terrors buried deep within me, flaring up whenever I dwelled on them. At breakfast time he tried to persuade me to eat a little porridge again, I had a few small spoonfuls of the soft, slimy oats, but no more than that. He took my temperature every three hours, it hovered between 39°C and 40°C all day, my body engulfed in a cold sweat, freezing.

In the afternoon he came up to my room with a bowl of mashed banana and a spoon, and immediately I felt like a child again. He looked concerned, my temperature had increased.

Shall I call the doctor? he asked.

No, it'll pass. I just need a few days.

What is it?

Flu, I think.

Who could you have caught it from?

It feels like flu.

He stood up and opened the window. My teeth chattered.

We just need a little fresh air in here.

I nodded. Took a sip of juice. I felt awful, yet so pleased to have this kind of access to him. I hoped I'd never be well again.

He sat down.

Is there anything I can do for you?

No.

If your fever hasn't come down by tomorrow, we're calling the doctor.

I accepted his statement with a nod.

He stroked my forehead.

You're soaking wet.

I nodded.

He paused for a moment.

Are your pyjamas damp?

I nodded.

He stood up.

I'll pop them in the washing machine.

He stood at the door then walked out of the room. It was all so vague. I pulled my pyjama top over my head, my arms and legs aching. I threw the top and trousers across the room, both landing just by the door. A moment later he popped his head around the door, glanced down and leaned over to pick them up. Here, he said, throwing a piece of fabric in my direction and closing the door behind him. I picked up the nightdress, it was grey, soft cotton, and I felt relieved that it was such an everyday, comfortable item, had feared she might have worn sensual, flowing silk garments that I'd never be able to carry off with any dignity. I pulled the nightdress over my head and stuck my arms through the sleeves, then lay back down.

The room was in complete darkness. He was sitting by the desk.

You're dreaming.

Am I?

No, you're awake now, Allis. But a moment ago.

I can't remember a thing.

You were afraid.

Is it night time?

Yes.

He was sitting in a strange light, the room spinning around him. My stomach felt hollow, but I wasn't hungry.

Are you really here?

Yes, he said. I'm here.

We were silent. I felt yet another feverish shiver creep over me, scraping my way through the trembling convulsions. He came over and tucked the duvet more snugly around me, then sat back down.

What's happened to you? I heard my own voice mumble, sounding peculiar, muffled.

He hesitated.

What have you done, Sigurd?

It was my voice, but it was so distant.

I saw him turn to face me, looking down. His head was bowed, his posture crooked, the moon shining on the back of his neck.

He paused, breathed deeply, paused again.

I need to know, I heard my voice mumble, confused. I felt myself disappearing, sinking back into sleep.


It was just beginning to grow light outside, not a single sound to be heard. He was still sitting there.

Can you tell me something, Sigurd?

Tell you what? he asked, expressionless.

A story.

Silence. I heard him draw breath.

It was summertime, five years ago, he eventually began. The hottest summer that I can remember. We swam out from the jetty every day in July. It was unreal, that's the only word that I can think of to describe it; it was impossible to do anything: we couldn't work, we could barely be bothered to eat. One day we were down by the jetty from morning all the way through to the evening, swimming, sunbathing, sitting in the shade then swimming all over again. Our bodies were burning by the time evening fell, we lay on the wall at sunset with a bottle of calvados, drunk and happy and dizzy with joy.

He stopped.

Calvados, I thought.

I braided her hair down by the jetty, it was thick after swimming in the salty water. I always did that for her, especially before she played a concert, she wasn't all that good at doing it herself. Then we decided to take the rowboat out. We had an old, beautiful *Oselvar*, a little traditional three-strake *færing*. As dusk fell, we picked up a fishing rod and pushed the boat out into the shallows, staggering all the while. I can remember her laughing behind me as I took an unsteady step and almost tripped over trying to clamber inside.

She rowed. She loved to row, her arms were strong and each stroke of the oars was long and slow. Outside the boat everything was still, the land and sea breezes had died down, the sun had dropped behind the mountain. We spoke in hushed tones so nobody in the cabins looking out onto the fjord would hear us, chuckling under our breath at each other. We sat like that in the twilight, me with the fishing rod, her with the oars, the most perfectly still night. The heat was finally beginning to subside.

I lay there, listening to his muffled voice, breathing as quietly as I knew how, not wanting to cut him off, not wanting to remind him that I was lying there. Concerts, I thought, she was a musician; how could I even begin to compete with something like that.

Of course, the conditions were all wrong for fishing, but I took the rod out for my own amusement more than anything, he continued.

But then the rod was tugged from my grasp, right out of nowhere, it must have been a huge fish, and out of pure instinct I leapt after it before it was dragged over the gunwale. Nor rose up just as instinctively, but the oars slipped from her grasp, she fell back, hit her head against the gunwale, everything happened so quickly. Suddenly she was under, in the black water, and I dived in but I couldn't see her, had to come up to the surface again and again. And then finally I caught sight of her, way down below me, and I swam to her, pulled her up, heaved her into the boat, the oars floating away across the water all the while, and she just lay there as I swam out to fetch them, and I had no idea whether to row us back to land or try to resuscitate her then and there, out in the middle of the fjord ... I was frantic, rowing us towards land, but even as I did so I knew that I'd made the wrong decision, Nor lying lifeless as I heaved at the oars, so I stopped, tried to resuscitate her in the boat, but I changed my mind and started rowing again, and every decision I made was wrong. Eventually I managed to get her breathing again, and help arrived, but such a long time had already passed. She was in the hospital for so long.

My God.

After a few months she was transferred from a hospital to a nursing home. There was nothing to do but wait for her to come round.

My heart raced, I was frozen, felt a lump in my throat. And then what?

He didn't reply.

Then what?

Then, time passed. Nothing happened. She wouldn't wake up.

He sat in silence for a long while.

And then?

Nothing. Not until the phone call two weeks ago. She'd taken a turn for the worse. I had to decide whether they could retrieve her organs.

I let out a gasp.

And?

That was that. I went in. Sat with her for a day, then a night, and another day after that. He faltered for a moment. And then it was time.

I'll stay here as long as you want me to, I said, and closed my eyes.

The sun was warm on my face. I sat up in bed. My body was trembling slightly, my back stiff and sore. I rolled my shoulders back, my joints no longer ached. I had sweated out the last of the fever. I stood up and walked over to the window. The sun was shining brightly on the milky-white blooms of the cherry tree down below. I opened the window and felt a gentle breeze against my skin. The morning was sparkling-bright and mild. I took a deep breath. I heard the snapping of twigs in the forest and the sound of birds taking flight, flapping between the branches.

A new world.

I saw him walking up the steps from the jetty, his fishing rod in one hand. He looked up at me, then stopped and raised a hand, carrying on through the garden and stopping under my window.

How are you feeling?

Better, thanks.

He smiled at me, looking relieved.

Catch anything?

Nothing.

He stayed where he was and looked up at me, standing at the window in his wife's nightdress. I gazed down at him. He drew breath as if to say something but instead just smiled. A certain reticence had come over him. He stood there, fishing rod in hand. I wasn't sure how to let him know that I remembered everything he had told me, that I had taken it all in. I stood there looking down at him, leaned forward slightly. He looked up at me with surprise. I nodded, gravely, then stepped away from the window.

Just a few days earlier we had been up the ladder picking the last of the apples. Now, all of a sudden, there were tiny, dry flakes of snow in the air. I gathered the dirty laundry and made my way down to the cellar. Something dashed past out of the corner of my eye as I set the laundry basket down on the hard stone floor. I froze, listening intently. I was convinced that I could hear a rustling. I crouched down, leaning in close to the wall. They had managed to chew their way through; I could see a small, uneven gap in the floor in the corner. I bounded up the stairs and to the kitchen cupboard under the sink, where the steel wool was kept. How many could there be? They could be all over the house, disgusting. I stuffed the hole with steel wool and studied the wall, searching for any more gaps. For all I knew, there was a mouse nest tucked away in the insulation; the thought sent shivers down my spine. Behind the washing machine I found mouse droppings. There were more along the wall under the row of hooks where Bagge's oil-skins and work clothes were hanging. As I pushed the clothing aside to check for more gaps, a door handle came into view. It had never occurred to me that there might be a door here, but it suddenly seemed obvious; this room was just one small part of the cellar. I could almost feel the mice scurrying over my feet and I shuddered, pushed on the handle and used every ounce of my strength to shove the door open. It must have been sealed shut for a long time.

On the other side of the door was nothing but a cold, empty cellar space. It was dark, I fumbled towards the light switch, but the light wouldn't come on. I was convinced that I could hear mice scampering along by the walls and around my feet. I held my breath. By the outer wall I glimpsed part of a staircase and a door, the door leading down to the cellar, of course, the one by the veranda that I hadn't spent any time thinking about before now. I wasn't supposed to be here. The bulb above me had been unscrewed. I screwed the bulb back into place

and tried the light once more, it flickered a few times before dying.
The cellar was empty, damp, and at the opposite end of the room was
a small staircase leading up to the ceiling at an angle. I took a few hesitant steps towards it, constantly fearful I might step on something soft,
thinking about how my weight would cause the thin skin to rip open.
The staircase led to a trapdoor in the ceiling, I felt my way towards it
with fumbling hands. A trapdoor. I tried to orientate myself, which
room was above me, his bedroom, his workroom? Almost like a timid
greeting, I knocked at the trapdoor, then again, a little more insistently
this time. Nothing. He had gone in there after breakfast, but perhaps
he was sleeping. No, not after breakfast. I pressed my palms against the
trapdoor and pushed, lifting it upwards.

Hello?

I pushed it all the way open and stood with my head sticking
through the hole in the floor. The room was empty, nothing there but
a window, a door, a chair, a cardboard box and an instrument case
propped up in the corner. There were several dark rectangular marks
on the wall directly opposite me, left where pictures had once been
hanging. I climbed up the final few steps. Bagge's workroom.

I sneaked over and looked at the case, a violin case. His wife's. A
folded-up music stand lay on the floor behind the cardboard box. I
opened the box: sheet music. My stomach twitched so violently that I
found myself doubled over. A sob slipped out. A prickling sensation,
white spots before my eyes.

Hurriedly I made my way back downstairs as quickly and quietly as
I could, the sound of my pulse thudding in my ears. No desk, no tools
of any kind, nothing but a violin. Did he play? No, impossible, I'd have
heard him. There in that empty room, that's where he spent those long
hours, day in and day out. I crouched down, squeezed my eyes tightly
closed, wishing that I hadn't seen the things I just had. The fact that
the room was as good as empty was more upsetting than anything else.
Almost anything would have been better. I pictured him sitting on
the floor, brooding, leaning against the wall by the violin case, staring
vacantly ahead, agonising over his situation. Sitting there, thinking

about his wife – the thought pained me, like a knife to the gut. And where was he now? In his bedroom? Was that where he spent his time? Each and every day, besides those he had been away, he had gone to his workroom after every meal, which he accessed through his bedroom, and he would stay there, saying he was working on something, that this was the reason he needed help around the house and in the garden. But now? I could never say what I knew. I hurried into the laundry room and loaded the machine.

I forced myself to take slow, deep breaths, again and again. It was almost one o'clock. I tried to steady my arms, my trembling fingers causing the plates to clatter, knives clinking against glasses as I set the table. I slammed the condiments down on the table. On the stroke of one, his door opened and he stepped out of the room just as I was moving between the worktop and the table, and I found myself frozen there, like a deer in headlights. I quickly turned to the worktop and clutched the teapot.

It's ready.

Good.

He sat down. I poured him a cup of tea, my arm outstretched, the stream of boiling liquid missing his cup and dribbling into the saucer.

We ate in silence. I spent most of the meal looking down, trying to breathe normally, calmly, something that felt impossible. My breath caught in my throat, I wanted to divulge what I knew. He said nothing, behaved just like his normal self, but still I felt him watching me. Eventually he placed his knife down on his plate and cleared his throat.

Is something wrong?

No?

You're very quiet.

There are mice in the cellar, I eventually muttered.

Bloody hell, Bagge hissed. It was the first time that I had heard him use such strong language, his words shook me.

Do we have any traps?

No, unfortunately not.

Then I'll go out and buy some, I said, swiftly and decisively pushing my chair out from under the table. He looked up at me with some surprise as I strode past him and over to the veranda door, looking out, acting as if there was something that I needed to check, then turning and looking at the back of his head to check his hair, to see if he had been lying in his bed. It looked as it always did. I pulled on some extra layers and made my way to the bus stop.

I returned with forty traps. Better too many than too few. Each and every one of those mice was sentenced to death, not a single one was to be allowed to survive the winter. I placed half of the traps along the outside walls of the house, by the wood stack and in the tool shed, then the rest on the three floors of the house, most of them ending up down in the cellar. They were ordinary snap traps with steel springs – guillotines for tiny rodents. Bagge took great interest in my extermination operation, regularly asking for updates, and the fact pleased me. At night I dreamed of mice, checking each trap, gathering great heaps of mouse corpses.

The bait lay untouched in each of the traps for the first few days. I had stuffed every nook and cranny with steel wool. Even so, I knew they were there, inside and out. I had no idea how many there could be. I sneaked down into the cellar at the strangest of hours, as if to catch them off guard, acting as if I had errands to run. Silently I would creep down, pausing on the second-to-last step and flicking the switch at lightning speed—! But no. Nothing.

A blurry shadow bolted past as I stepped out of the bathroom, only to vanish into thin air. The rodents must have had another crack in the wall that I hadn't found, or else this one had managed to sneak in under the door to the sealed-off room filled with his wife's things. I inspected the wall where the mouse had disappeared but I couldn't see a thing. I lay down flat on the floor and listened at various spots all the way along the wall. In the furthest corner I was sure I could hear a faint, almost inaudible squeaking – either that, or I was going mad. I sprinted down to Bagge's room and knocked at his door, but there was no answer. I took a deep breath, opened the door and looked inside. He wasn't there. Feeling emboldened and well within my rights, I crossed the room and grabbed the door handle. The door opened onto the empty workroom, the trapdoor inside flush with the floor. I bristled with palpable, prickling wrath, a combination of disgust at the mice and anger at the way he'd tricked me.

I ran outside and across the garden, pulled the crowbar from the wall of the tool shed, returned inside and ran upstairs. I put all of my weight behind the crowbar and eventually the plank of wood gave way with a loud creak. There they were, in the insulation, nestled away like a mass of transparent, rosy-pink testicles. I shuddered, motionless, indecisive, unable to settle on a plan of action. The tiny clumps of skin squirmed slowly, silently, blindly squeaking in my direction. Should I burn them, bury them, execute them one by one – and if so, how? Using what? I didn't know what options were available to me, each seemed uglier than the last.

I slid the plank of wood back into position by the nest to prevent them from scurrying off or calling for reinforcements, then ran downstairs and knocked at Bagge's door again.

Hello! Hello! Sigurd!

I poked my head out of the door leading to the garden and called out to him. I slipped my feet into my boots, stepped out onto the veranda and peered out. I saw tracks in the snow crossing the lawn, leading from the cellar door down through the garden. I followed them, not bothering to fetch a coat first, the snow drifting down, gathering in my hair and at the nape of my neck, tracing the footsteps through the white garden and further on, down the steps to the jetty, where they stopped in front of the boathouse. I didn't dare do anything, didn't dare call out to him. But I knew he'd realise I had been here when he finally emerged, provided the snow hadn't covered my tracks by then.

I could hear muffled scraping sounds coming from inside the boathouse. Fine. OK. He worked in there. The boathouse was his bolthole; how could I have missed that until now? I suddenly recalled all of the times he'd come up from the jetty without me ever having seen him emerge from his room. It was so obvious now that he had been leaving through the cellar door. But why? I had to make my presence known. I stepped up to the door and knocked firmly, then took a step back. Waited.

Sigurd!

I waited, taking another deep breath.

Sigurd!

The scraping inside came to a halt. The door opened and he peered out. He glared at me, his face red, his hair damp, clad only in a light shirt in spite of the cold.

Sorry, but I—

What is it?

I've found a mouse nest in one of the walls upstairs.

He ducked behind the door and re-emerged wearing his coat. I followed him up the steps and planned what I'd say in case he pulled me up for cracking open the walls of his house.

I'll take care of it, he said as we stepped inside.

But what will you do?

Don't worry about it.

I took this as a clear order to keep my distance, so I lingered in the kitchen and started placing ingredients on the kitchen counter. I heard a few sharp slams from the attic, then he came back downstairs. I didn't turn around to look at him as he marched through the hallway and out of the door at the back of the house. Not long afterwards he came in to see me.

There.

Is it done?

It's done.

He smiled and I gave him an appreciative nod.

Good.

By the way, he continued, can you come up here for a minute?

We climbed the stairs. He had nailed the plank I had pulled away back into place, but the door to the room filled with his wife's things was open.

I had forgotten all about this lot. Nor's things, he said, everything in these boxes here. Please, see if there's anything here that you like, anything you think you might be able to get some use out of.

Are you sure that's what you want?

Of course, Allis. Otherwise it'll all just sit here.

He went downstairs and I held back, hesitant, then stepped inside and looked around. Slowly I opened the box closest to me. The clothes inside had been neatly folded. There were fine wool jumpers, silk blouses, skirts, dresses, every item simple and elegant, high-quality garments in pretty shades. Such beautiful taste. She had bought sophisticated clothing, played concerts, strolled through town with her instrument case slung over her shoulder, high heels and silk blouses beneath a longline camel hair coat, laughing as she made her way to orchestra practice, drinking coffee with her fellow musicians in the cafe at the art gallery; an enchanting figure with dark, wavy hair, eyes sparkling with life, enfolded in Bagge's arms as evening fell.

At around five o'clock, I went downstairs and started on dinner. I browned meat and braised root vegetables, sprinkled red wine over everything and placed the casserole dish in the oven on a low heat. I assumed that he'd gone back down to the boathouse. His workroom obviously functioned as his passage down there. Now I knew that, and he knew that I knew, if he didn't voluntarily offer an explanation then it would be natural for me to bring it up. I had so few clues as to what he might be doing that my imagination was unable to come up with a single suggestion, though it had sounded like some kind of woodwork.

Checking on the meat before dinner I found him standing in the kitchen. He was straight out of the shower, steam still lingering around him.

This'll be ready in ten minutes.

Then I'll go downstairs and fetch us a bottle.

I set the table and made my way upstairs to change. When I came back down, he was already sitting at the table. He blinked when he caught sight of me, a momentary double-take. Self-conscious and immediately regretful, I approached him, the dress clinging to every curve.

Was it wrong of me?

No. You look beautiful.

I placed the casserole dish on the table and passed him the ladle. He helped himself as I carefully swirled the wine around inside my glass, waiting for him to taste the food.

Wow, he declared softly, leaning back in his chair.

Tender?

He nodded and carried on chewing. I helped myself from the steaming dish. We ate in silence, sipping our wine, snow still falling outside. I felt ashamed to be sitting there in his wife's dress, but it had looked so beautiful in the mirror and had fitted me so perfectly, the shimmering, blue-green material almost the colour of a mallard's head.

As he ate, he looked up at me again, but differently from before. He was staring at me. My cheeks were flushed. Here I am, I thought to myself, dressed as his wife. I changed my mind and swore to myself that I wouldn't ask about the boathouse, wouldn't risk the prospect of his anger flaring up yet again.

The casserole dish was empty. He had polished off everything and looked up at me with an expression bordering on disbelief. He stood up before I managed to do so.

Stay where you are, I'll take care of this.

He picked up the plates and cutlery and carried everything to the sink.

Coffee?

Yes, please.

After he had poured our coffee and taken his seat once again, silence descended on us.

Do you think you'll stay here for the rest of your life? I heard myself ask quite suddenly.

I do, he replied, as if it were nothing. I'm certain of it.

But don't you need to work?

Do you think I don't work?

I don't know. Do you?

He peered at me over the rim of his coffee cup, eyes of quartz.

I didn't mean to... I began. But ... I happened to find the trapdoor leading to your workroom. When I was hunting for mice. I wasn't sneaking around.

Hunting for mice? Are you a cat now?

I didn't know where the stairs led, I just wanted to...

And you found yourself in an empty room.

I thought you said a while back that you were a lawyer?

A lawyer?

Law and order, that's what you told me when I asked about your work.

His eyes softened.

Oh, Allis. You remember everything. I can't say anything to you.

I didn't mean to—

I'm sorting things out down in the boathouse. But you're not allowed to see, not until I'm finished. I promise that you can see it then.

Why won't you let me see?

You'd only be disappointed as things are.

He stood up.

A little port would go down nicely now, don't you think?

I do.

He stopped in the middle of the room on his way to the cellar door.

Allis.

Yes?

Do you think you'll stay here for the rest of your life, too?

Yes. I think I will, I replied, startled by my own words. The briefest hint of a smile flickered across his lips before he disappeared down the stairs. A sudden calm washed over me. He returned with the port, found two glasses in the cupboard and poured a little for us both.

He stood behind me after he had set the bottle down, his large, warm hands on my shoulders, the smooth fabric of the dress, holding them there calmly without a word. He gathered my hair in his hands, running his fingers through it before starting to braid. His rough fingers brushed gently against the nape of my neck, then he laid the plait over my left shoulder and turned me around to face him. He looked at me. Perhaps he caught a glimpse of something in my eyes.

Don't be afraid, he said, cupping my face in his hands. He crouched down in front of me. I don't think that you're her.

No, I said, a sickly sorrow languishing in the pit of my stomach.

I don't, he repeated. He leaned forward and kissed me tenderly, then ran his fingers through the braid, so my hair hung loose down my back.

You're Allis.

I nodded.

Come with me.

I still had my room in the attic if I wanted to read or spend some time alone, but I slept in Bagge's room. The house was cold at night, but his bed was warm. Sometimes he lay with his back to me, sometimes with an arm wrapped around me. I was still the first to get up each day to make breakfast; he would come in afterwards and we'd eat together.

After breakfast he would step into his boots, pull a thick jumper over his head and make his way down to the boathouse. I wandered between the trees, red-cheeked and runny-nosed, shaking the branches free from the wet, heavy snow to prevent damage, the same for the bushes too. There was very little to do in the garden. I spent my days tidying the tool shed, cleaning the tools carefully and sweeping up and throwing away any debris; I'd taken February at its word, the month the Etruscans named after the god of the underworld and purification. There were occasional periods of mild weather before the springtime chill would strike back without warning. I had tied fat balls to the branches of the cherry tree by the veranda, each one teeming with tiny birds that I'd watch for hours at a time from the window.

There were signs of spring beginning to emerge. I took cuttings from the trees outside and placed them in warm water, apple and cherry blossoms flourishing on the windowsills indoors.

I finished sorting through Nor's things for anything that I wanted to keep, and had moved all of my clothes into his room. The rest had been packed back into boxes, which he had left in a skip behind the shop. I wondered whether things could really be like this, like they were now. I believed it was possible. Our days revolved around good food, reading, gardening, making love on occasion. In the evenings we would sit in our chairs, reading and stoking the fire, quietly discussing the snowfall, the snowdrops, the spring.

She surveyed me with a particular intensity having left me to my own devices for so long. The shelves were barer than ever, the vegetable section now little more than a few sparsely populated crates of root vegetables and the odd apple. I studied every onion with great care before placing it in my basket; on several occasions I had come home only to discover that they were mouldy beneath the outer layers. She peered at me brazenly wherever I roamed. It would soon be worthwhile taking the bus all the way into town to do my shopping, just to avoid this. I could build up a supply of dry goods with each trip, sacks of beans, lentils, grains and rice, and we could be self-sufficient in the future, at least as far as the majority of our vegetables were concerned. I could make contact with local hunters, buy meat directly from them, get eggs and milk from local farmers. Go fishing every day. I'd be more than happy to return to a system of bartering, but I would need something to exchange in return for what we needed.

A new coat, I see, she remarked as I placed my items on the counter. It suits you.

I was wearing Nor's long, grey, woollen winter coat, somehow I hadn't realised as I had prepared to leave the house.

Thank you. You certainly have a keen eye.

I see lots of things, you know.

Her frizzy, yellow hair lay flat against her pink scalp. A prickling sensation crept over me.

Yes, apparently so.

I took my change and lifted the bags from the counter.

Tell that foul *nithing* I send my best.

I stopped in my tracks, then turned and looked her in the eye.

What did you say?

Send my regards when you see him next.

Her gaze was unwavering as she stared back at me, the merest trace of a sneer on her face.

I longed to rush down to him in the boathouse but I didn't want to disturb him. I waited until I saw him at dinner. When I told him what she had said, he stopped chewing. He raised his eyebrows as he lifted his glass and took a long swig.

Did she say anything else?

No, just that.

I omitted her comment about the coat. He said nothing.

So—

Don't dwell on it, he said, picking up his knife and fork and carrying on eating.

After dinner I made my way around the house to check the mouse traps. All twenty traps throughout the house were empty. I took my torch and ventured outside. The first two traps by the wood stack were empty, too, but as I neared the tool shed, I spotted two dark shadows in the traps, and my heart leapt. I hurried over to survey my catch, but the cone of light from my torch came to rest not on a mouse, but a great tit.

No, I murmured, hurrying to check the next trap: yet another great tit, nailed in place by the hard steel spring.

I didn't know what to do. I stood up and walked around to the other side of the house to check the traps I had laid around there. Another two great tits, with a blue tit clamped to death in a third. Around the corner were two empty traps, with another great tit caught in a third. I counted seven empty traps and thirteen birds all in all, each lying flat with their black eyes wide open.

Unnerved by my discovery, I checked the bookshelves for a book or encyclopaedia or anything that might offer some suggestions as to what I could place in the traps that wouldn't attract small birds.

What is it? Sigurd asked.

There are birds caught in the traps.

No mice?

No, just piles of mangled great tits.

He placed his book down in his lap.

What did you put in the traps?

Fat.

Try some sweet fruit, mice will go for that.

Fruit?

Or you could hang up a large nesting box at the edge of the forest and see if you can persuade a tawny owl to nest there. There are no better mice hunters, and there are plenty of tawny owls out there in the forest.

Really?

Have you buried the birds?

I looked down.

They're still in the traps. I...

He picked up his book.

It's just part of the job, he said with a stern expression.

That night I dreamt about the great tits, which I had laid to rest in a mass grave behind the wood stack before going to bed. In my dream, dead great tits were scattered everywhere I went, piled up in corners of the house, filling the bathtub, their eyes wide open, their shaggy little necks limp, their small heads and tiny beaks drooping, lifeless. I was wearing the shimmering green dress, cycling along the main road without a bicycle light, and tiny birds filled the ditches lining the road, mounds of their bodies littering my path, impossible to avoid running over as I cycled. When I entered the shop, she was stationed behind the counter as usual, an eagle mask covering her face.

In the middle of the night I was woken by sounds downstairs. I was alone in the bed. I heard the door close. It was almost four o'clock in the morning. He returned to the bedroom soon after, undressing and sliding under the bed covers. I tried as best I could to breathe normally, inconspicuously. His chest rose and fell hard and fast, and as I lay with my back to him, I could see the outline of the shadow he cast against the wall. What on earth was he doing outside at this time of night? There was a demonic glow about him. He reminded me of White Bear King Valemon from the fairy-tale. He placed an arm around me. I felt his warm breath on my neck and I grew calm.

I took my bicycle and wheeled it through the forest and up to the main road. When I arrived, I was surprised to find the shop in darkness, closed to customers. I let out a triumphant sigh. There wouldn't be any fruit for my mouse traps after all, but at least I might have met her prying, eagle-eyed gaze for the last time. I turned around and cycled home, leaning over my handlebars, straight-backed, inwardly delighted, bolstered by a sensation of justice having been served.

He was standing in the garden when I trundled back down towards the house, axe in one hand and a small pile of freshly chopped wood behind him.

The shop was closed.

Oh?

But we have everything we need, at least for another few days. Do you want some help stacking that?

Please.

I brought the wheelbarrow over and started to fill it.

It was always a horrible experience shopping there, anyway, never knowing what she was going to say next.

Yes, he said. She won't be troubling you anymore.

He grasped the handles of the wheelbarrow and rolled it neatly between the pile and where I stood, then I stacked each log soundly in place. The occasional snowflake fluttered in the air around us, the last of the winter snow. I carried an armful of logs into the house and lit the fire.

The April mornings were still cold. After breakfast we made our way outside, hats on and garden shears in hand. He pruned the fruit trees while I took care of the berry shrubs. He circled each tree again and again, carefully trimming selected branches one by one. Afterwards we raked up the branches and twigs and I rolled everything away in the wheelbarrow. When I returned, he was strolling along by the stone wall, on his way to the vegetable patch.

In the evening, he sipped a cup of tea in the kitchen as I chopped up root vegetables for baking in the oven.

But what happened to Hermód? he asked, setting his mug down.

Hermód?

Don't you remember telling me the story of Balder? Hermód rode to Hel to offer her a ransom for Balder. To have him released from the underworld and sent back to Asgard. Remember?

Ah, Hermód. You have a good memory.

I had to think for a moment.

He rides for nine nights straight in pitch darkness, I said, sitting down at the table. Over Gjallarbrú, the bridge crossing the river Gjöll, and all the way to the gates of Helheim. He spurs Sleipnir and they leap over the gate. He dismounts and walks inside to find Balder seated on a throne.

His brother.

Yes. Hermód explains to Hel why he has come. He recounts the grief felt by gods and mankind in the wake of Balder's death. He tells her that he has come on behalf of Frigg to beg Hel to allow him to take Balder home to Asgard. Hel agrees on one condition: she demands that everything in the world weep for Balder, whether living or dead. If every creature weeps, he'll be allowed to return, but if even one fails to do so, Balder will have to remain there with her. Balder follows Hermód out and gives him Draupnir to pass on to Odin as a gift.

Hermód rides home to Asgard with Hel's message, and the gods send word to all the creatures in the world, begging them to weep until Balder is freed from Helheim. Every creature promises to do so apart from one old giantess who goes by the name of Thökk. When the gods' messenger asks her to cry for Balder, she replies: Thökk will shed dry tears over Balder's cremation. Let Hel keep what she has.

Loki, he whispered.

Yes.

And Balder is forced to remain there with Hel.

Yes.

So what about Loki?

Loki is discovered and tortured. They bind him with his own son's entrails, which turn to iron. They hang a serpent above him, which drips venom onto his face, causing him excruciating pain. Loki's wife Sigyn holds a small bowl over him to catch the venom before it falls onto his face, but whenever it becomes full she is forced to empty it, and the venom drips onto Loki's face once again. He writhes around so violently that the whole world shakes, causing earthquakes.

She should have left him to take his punishment.

Everyone wishes him ill; he has no one. I think it's poignant.

He cast me a dark glance.

It's easy to love Balder. Everybody did. But imagine loving Loki, I said.

She's hindering his atonement.

I took a deep breath.

I'd do the same for you, I replied, blushing as I uttered the words.

He flashed another glance at me then growled something and turned around, hastily pulling on his boots and storming out of the house. Without a word he tramped across the veranda and left me gaping, his large, strong back disappearing further down the garden. I had never said anything finer to any man, and this was my only thanks. I gathered the vegetable peel with agitated sweeps. He was being so unfair, what kind of response was that? I had left myself vulnerable and his only reaction was to leave.

I roughly scrubbed the chopping board, rinsed and wrung out the cloth then made my way up to my room and sank down onto the bed. There were still a good few hours before my usual bedtime, but I decided to stay there until then. He could mull things over, sleep alone and have a good think about his behaviour. I lay motionless, eyes squeezed tightly shut, all of my remaining senses heightened.

A little after eleven I heard him downstairs. Footsteps, then a pause, and a few more back the way. Faltering. Irritating. He stepped into his bathroom. A little afterwards I heard him moving around again, closing his bedroom door behind him. I flipped over where I lay, my face buried in my pillow, sobbing with indignation. Just a few choked sobs, each one brief, then a deep breath before I managed to successfully summon sleep.

He was already sitting at the table when I arrived downstairs the following morning. Throughout my childhood and adolescent years, and now, even in adulthood, my irrational pride prevented me from ever taking the initiative when it came to reconciliation, ever. I walked by without looking at him or saying a word, taking a mug from the cupboard and pouring myself a cup of coffee before sitting down. It was up to him.

Allis.

I looked at him.

I'm sorry.

The knot inside me loosened slightly, I took his hand.

So am I.

Look, he said, turning around to glance behind him. He picked up a large, pale-coloured box, just over half a metre in height. There was a large hole in the front.

It's a tawny owl nesting box. For your mice.

Is it really?

We can hang it today. If you'd like to, that is.

I would.

It needs to be up high, so it'll take both of us.

I lifted the box, the edges of the light wood perfectly smooth, then opened the lid and looked inside, the base covered in a layer of sawdust, ready for moving into.

Did you make it yesterday?

He nodded.

It might be too late in the spring to attract any owls straight away, but we can try.

Thirty metres into the forest, Bagge stopped. We lowered the ladder onto the forest floor.

Here, he said.

The pine tree was tall. The forest around wasn't too dense.

Do you want to, or shall I?

You, I replied.

He tied the rope around the box. We lifted the ladder up, balancing it against the tree trunk, then he picked up the end of the rope and started to climb. I held the ladder for safety. I saw how the damp rubber soles of his boots could slip on a rung, my stomach churning as I watched him sail through the air and hit his head on—

Allis! You need to let go of the rope!

Of course. Sorry.

He carried on climbing. He was three or four metres above me.

Isn't that high enough?

My heart slammed all the harder, sick at the sight of him so high above me.

Five metres, he called to me. I stared straight ahead at the tree trunk in front of me, gripping the ladder so firmly that my knuckles turned white. The ladder juddered in my hands with every step he took.

Now, Allis!

I looked up. He was balancing on one of the topmost rungs, more than half of his body hovering unsupported above the ladder, one arm wrapped around the trunk for balance.

Send the box up!

I reached for the box without letting go of the ladder, terrified of stumbling over something, the thought putting me off the task at hand. He started to pull the box up with his end of the rope. He was a tiny speck above me in the pine tree. I couldn't watch as he started securing the box to the tree. The ladder shook, rocking back and forth, and I leant up against it with all of my weight, trying my best to stabilise it. It stopped shuddering. I looked up. He looked down at me with a peculiar expression.

He said nothing.

I gazed up at him.

What is it?

He let go of the tree and stood there, balancing on the fourth rung from the top.

I'm going to jump.

You need to be higher for anything like that! I cried impulsively.

He started to laugh, surprised by my outburst.

You're right about that.

He climbed down. When he reached the ground, he put his arms around me. I had broken out in a quivering, cold sweat.

He stroked my hair, chuckling softly, then let go and pointed upwards: This time next year you'll have an owl for a neighbour.

You know the tawny owl's call is considered a death omen?

Yes, death to the mice, he replied.

We walked through the forest together afterwards. I was keen to see if the first wood anemones had emerged. He followed me.

A white light glittered in a clearing in the distance, and we walked towards it. As we got closer, I realised it was the same area I'd stumbled upon the previous year, the open clearing in the middle of the forest where I had found the black circle. He stopped as I approached it. I turned to face him.

What happened here?

Here?

There must have been a fire.

Perhaps you're right.

I crouched down. He walked towards me. I ran both hands over the ground until I found something, picking it up.

A nail.

Yes, he replied.

I searched again, finding two, three, four more. Each was black with soot.

Somebody must have burned some old building materials here.

He stood there, silent.

There are more nails over here.

They're not just nails, Allis. They're copper boat nails.

Copper boat nails?

They're used for fastening planks together on boats.

I looked at him with astonishment, saying nothing as I waited for him to continue. He didn't appear to have anything weighing on his mind. I stood up.

Your wood anemones are over here, he said, pointing at a small mound of earth bathed in sunlight, white amidst the surrounding green. They were wet with dew, I crouched down and picked a small bunch. A tangible silence had come between us.

Shall we head back?

Wait a minute, he said.

I stopped. He was standing in the middle of the black patch of earth, flecks of sunlight and shadow on his face.

It's the boat. He turned to look at me. I burned my boat here.

But, why?

He said nothing.

Because of the accident?

He nodded.

But how did you get it all the way up here?

I dragged it.

Dragged it? Through the whole forest?

He shook his head.

Up through the garden.

What?

Up the steps, through the garden and then here.

I don't believe you. A boat? It's too heavy.

He said nothing.

Why did you do it?

He gave no reply.

Why did you burn the boat?

I didn't want it.

Was this long ago?

Just after the accident.

You pulled it up here all by yourself?

He nodded again.

But wasn't there an enquiry, after the accident, I mean? Didn't anybody come to investigate the scene?

I burned it after they came.

We both remained rooted to the spot.

You do too many strange things, I said. It frightens me.

He said nothing. Out of the corner of my eye his expression seemed distorted. He pulled the zip of his knitted pullover all the way up to his chin then stood there, composed and steadfast before me.

If I were as strange as you are, then maybe...

He turned around.

But I'm not. I'm actually quite normal.

His face softened.

Oh, he murmured. You're not normal.

I am, actually. I'm sorry if I've led you to think otherwise.

You and me, Allis, he said, smiling at me. Everything is different. You are here.

His tone was suddenly mild and carefree.

Shall we head back to the path?

I followed him through the forest, away from the site of the fire.

And what about after?

After what?

After you burned the boat, what did you do then?

He wrapped an arm around me and grasped my shoulder in his large hand.

I remember so little, almost nothing at all. Everything just fell apart. Before I knew it, years had passed.

What happened?

I woke up a year ago and looked around me. I had let the house fall into disrepair. I looked outside. Nor loved that garden but suddenly it was dying, just like she was. Even so, I couldn't bear to touch it, I would only have made matters worse there, too. I worked on fixing up the house inside and out, doing what was needed, but the garden was always just there. When I visited her, I told her about all of the plants that sprouted and grew there, thought that for as long as there was life in the garden, there might be life in her, too. But none of what I said was true. And gradually her condition worsened. So I sought help.

I felt a stab of guilt. Some help I was. If I had known, I might have made a more wholehearted attempt at honing my skills.

He stopped. Turned to look at me.

But then you came.

Exactly, I thought darkly, and what had I achieved since my arrival? I'd had a feeble dig around before engaging all of my efforts in running after Bagge.

He stroked my cheek, holding my chin for a moment before letting go. We carried on walking.

But that didn't help, he said. He took a deep breath.

That night of the eclipse, Allis. I'm so sorry about what happened.

Don't think about it.

I just felt as if I needed to get you away from me. As if it wasn't safe for you here, as if I'm the kind of person who destroys others.

You knew that I'd find my own way back.

No! he said. I was glad you'd managed to get away.

Don't say that.

He held me close and kissed the top of my head, gently blowing my hair.

We walked out of the forest with the pathway between us, strolling through the heather and down the bank to the garden. The spring sunshine lay low over the mountains, the sky pale yellow, the air perfectly clear.

You can't manage on your own, I said.

No.


The roasted joint rested on the kitchen bench. He was standing by the stove making a red-wine sauce.

If things are going to be like this... I began.

Yes?

If this is to be a household, I mean. Then we need to talk about certain things.

He nodded.

How we're going to get by.

He looked over at me.

For instance, I began, do we have any money?

You're the only outgoing.

You haven't paid me since August last year.

You haven't submitted any invoices, he replied, whisking in the tiny saucepan.

I was under the impression this was an under-the-table arrangement.

I set the meat to one side and poured the juices into his saucepan.

Perhaps I should look into going back to work. I have to, sooner or later.

Must you? he asked. I thought you worked for me now?

Oh ha ha – there's work and there's *work*.

Just how long does a scandal really last? I wondered to myself. Not long nowadays, people have enough of their own problems to worry about, and they move on so quickly, one scandal isn't enough, people need more, these things need to be topped up, the appetite for fresh shame is insatiable. This country is so tiny that nobody really dares to destroy anyone, not completely, anyway, just in part, because they know only too well that it could so easily be them instead.

Do you have any form of income? I asked.

He took the sieve from the drawer and strained the sauce into the gravy jug, saying nothing.

What do you actually do?

I can't say, he replied, a smooth trickle of deep-red sauce flowing into the gravy jug, and it was impossible to judge whether he found the entire conversation amusing or was being deadly serious.

Is that right?

He set down the saucepan and the sieve and cast me a long, contemplative look, one eyebrow raised, as if he doubted that I would understand what he had to say. Ex-military, perhaps, or a spy, the thought had occurred to me on occasion, something to do with the intelligence service, maybe. Suddenly it made me anxious, the fact he wouldn't share it with me.

Come on, just tell me! What is it, are you in a witness protection programme or something?

He locked eyes with me. A moment later his face cracked and he burst into laughter. I had read about witnesses getting cosmetic surgery, having their teeth extracted and all manner of things, all just to make themselves unrecognisable, and I had already conjured up an image of his real appearance, but now there were only near-silent peals of laughter, his head thrown back in mirth, before he eventually managed to suppress his amusement.

I'm sorry, he said. I'm only teasing you.

Well stop it.

I'm just afraid you'll lose interest in me once the mystery is finally solved.

I avoided eye contact. Part of me felt offended, but I'd often thought the same myself: what if it's the mystery that draws me to him? I forced myself to look up at him.

Idiot, I said.

Allis, he said, his tone grave. He set the gravy jug down on the table. You asked for this. It's your own fault if you're disappointed.

That's fine.

He inhaled.

I'm a joiner.

I looked at him. He gazed back at me with a solemn expression.

A joiner?

He nodded slowly.

Something swelled and sank within me all at once. Yes, if it were true then the mystery was over, but the shock was so great, the notion hadn't occurred to me even once. A manual labourer? What about his aristocratic air? Was I really standing face-to-face with a joiner, a humble joiner? It felt as if the dark sky above him paled as the hazy uncertainty that had lingered there faded away. But perhaps that was just as well. Only the gods knew how long I might have continued to tread on eggshells around him, terrified of making some obscure error or another. But now that he was a joiner, things were clearer, though I barely knew what that actually meant in practice; wasn't it some kind of carpentry? It was as if his status sank, I was forced to face up to the fact. I was better educated, a public persona, while he ... Oh dear, no. All of the good food I'd made him, all of the hours spent on homemade stock, convinced that I was preparing a meal of for some sort of nobleman, an earl, maybe, a man born with good taste, a man who would instantly be able to distinguish a bought stock from – ugh, all of my past efforts suddenly seemed so wasted. He had simply consumed whatever he had been presented with, no questions asked.

Are you surprised?

I had no idea, I said, trying to compose myself. I just hadn't ever seen you ... doing that. Not since I arrived here.

No, he said. But tomorrow we'll tackle those raised beds for the vegetable garden.

I told myself that I would embrace this new, less enigmatic version of him, that I'd be happy. After all, now he could teach me woodworking skills, we could go fishing together, work in the vegetable garden, have our own greenhouse, get a boat, set out nets, do everything it would take for us to get by out here.

I carved the meat and placed it on the table.

I did have work, he said, but after she fell ill, I needed a break. It was only supposed to be for a short while, but things didn't quite go to plan. Now that Nor has gone, maybe I can move forward somehow, get back to it, or...

For a moment I caught a glimpse of her, lying on the jetty in her bikini, slim-figured, her hair curled in a knot at the nape of her neck. I had to acknowledge that there was a certain consolation in doing so, a sense of security in knowing that he had been married; he must be OK, in spite of everything, the kind of man a woman could be with. I wasn't the only one to allow myself to be tricked into this, I didn't simply have low standards – he had been approved by an independent third party. Even so, when comparing myself with imaginary women, I tended to come off badly.

He gazed at me between the candlesticks. Could he tell when he looked at me? Did he realise just how superficial I was? That bizarre, frank realisation that you're quite suddenly living a normal life. But when it came down to it, perhaps there was nothing better. Wasn't that – exactly that – what I wanted? And wasn't it that which would be my salvation, the purest thing of all – an ordinary life without social ambition, a life of housework and gardening and reading, perhaps even starting a family? I looked at him. Here I was, I thought, as good as married to a joiner, a big, beautiful, brooding widower, a man of the forest with practical skills. It was a miracle.

A man of the forest, I said. It doesn't get much more erotic than that.

Exactly. Come here.

What?

Come and sit here.

I stood up and sat on his lap. He placed an arm around me and I breathed in his scent, burnt wood, rough sea, burying my nose in his hair, pressing it to his neck, his stubble scratching my cheek. A man of the forest.

I've wondered about you, he mumbles into my hair.

Wondered about me?

I was like stone before you came.

You were like stone long after I came, I said.

He smiled at my ear.

And you still are, I thought.

But then, he said.

Yes, what actually happened?

I wondered the same thing myself. Suddenly things were different. I wanted to be with you. Standing there in the kitchen, always there, even when you shouldn't have been.

Yes, I said. Yes. Wasn't that how it started? Suddenly you were there, you were with me.

That's right, he said, stroking a hand up and down my back.

There was something, I thought, a vague sensation that something wasn't quite right, but what was it exactly? I had been standing there chopping vegetables, adding fish to our bowls of soup, sprinkling herbs on top, all as he waited at the table. The realisation hit me like a cold, hard slam to the stomach. The blue book. The recipes. The smell of his wife's cooking.

Allis.

The food will stay warm for a while yet, I said.

He lifted me up.

Strange. So strange how anything is possible, I thought, as I floated across the room.

He came up from the boathouse as I watered the vegetable garden. The sun was searing; it had been dry for weeks. I was afraid the heat would finish off everything in the garden, and I watered the plants several times a day. He had a strange look about him, happy, carefree, he put an arm around me and kissed me. His hair was damp with sweat, his shirt clinging to his body.

Are you ready for lunch?

He nodded.

I picked a few salad leaves and some tomatoes and made us sandwiches in the kitchen. I baked bread every week. There still hadn't been anyone who'd come to take over the shop, but it made no odds, we took the bus into town whenever we needed anything. I had started reading up on keeping chickens and rabbits, seriously imagining the possibilities of meeting our needs in the long run, at least as far as meat was concerned.

We sat under the cherry tree. I had applied linseed oil to the chairs and table just a few days beforehand. The grass tickled the soles of my feet, the sun warming my legs.

It's too hot to work, I said.

Yes, he replied. He sighed and leaned back in his chair, his skin tanned, his face glistening.

Are things going well down in the boathouse?

He turned and looked at me, shading his eyes from the sun with a hand and smiling.

I just finished, actually.

Really?

He nodded, looking pleased with himself.

Can I come down and see?

Tomorrow, he said.

Why tomorrow?

There's just one more small thing that needs to be done.

Alright then, I'll wait.

He had been working down there almost every day for as long as I had been here, even back when I had believed he was in his workroom. I couldn't really understand what could take so long, especially not for someone for whom this was a job.

I moved into the shade of the cherry tree. The sun blazed. He leaned back in his chair, shirtless and dozing, pearls of sweat on his forehead and a piece of straw in his mouth. The branches of the shrubs behind him were laden with black and red berries. I glanced over towards the vegetable garden. It bustled with lettuce, radish, cabbage, herbs. I had spent all that morning earthing up the carrots and potatoes, laying planks between the rows to act as pathways. You hardly need me anymore, he had remarked as he had watched me work. I stole a glance at him, sleeping in the sunshine. I closed my eyes.

When I awoke, he was standing over me. The sky behind him was pale red.

An evening swim, he said. Is that totally off the cards for you?

Yes, but I'll watch.

Why don't you want to swim?

I just don't care for it. Never have.

Are you afraid of water?

No! I just prioritise my time differently from you.

He laughed. I walked with him down the stone steps to the jetty, perching myself on the warm wall. He undressed and jumped into the water.

Allis! he shouted from the water. It's so warm! You *have* to come in!

I laughed at him, shaking my head.

I'm just going up to fetch a book.

The freezer was filled with ice, I poured the lot into a bucket and opened a bottle of white wine, making room for two glasses and the bottle. I stuffed a blanket under one arm for later and strolled down towards the water. I couldn't see him, either on the jetty or in the fjord, he must be swimming further out. It left me with a deep-seated unease, the same I'd had since coming back, a sense that he needed looking after. Down by the jetty I placed the ice bucket on the ground and gazed out over the water, the fjord utterly still, not a single speck on the horizon. I didn't want to call out, so I bounded halfway up the stone steps to gain a better view, saw nothing, ran back down and simply stood there in bewilderment, gasping for breath, running to the edge, not knowing what else to do but to look for his head, his arms, out there. I was just about to pull my t-shirt over my head and dive in when the door of the boathouse opened and he strolled out wearing his trousers, a towel in one hand. He spotted the ice bucket and immediately brightened up. I turned around and smiled as if nothing had happened. He dried his back and sat down on the wall. It was only now that I noticed the wet footprints leading from the fjord to the boathouse; what a flustered idiot I was, forever jumping to the worst conclusions. I sat down beside him and poured a glass, passed it to him, then poured another for myself. We raised them silently in one another's direction. His hair was wet and glossy, so beautiful that it was painful to watch him as he sipped his wine and gazed out across the water. I exhaled. I lay back, the sun still lingering above the mountains, sure to be there for a few hours yet. A faint, faint breeze gave me goose bumps. So terrified, so relieved. He reached out to pick up his shirt and stuck his arms through the sleeves.

To think that it was you who came here, Allis.

Yes.

I turned around and buttoned up his shirt for him. Looked up at him.

But you never did tell me just how many applied.

He grinned and looked down.

You were the only one.

Really?

Of course. What kind of person would apply for such a job?

I would have thought there'd be at least a few more than that.

He shook his head.

Only you, you silly thing. He nudged me lightly with the back of his hand.

I suppose I am.

The sun rested just above the crest of the ridge. I glanced in his direction, bit my lip.

There's something I need to tell you.

What?

I didn't know all that much about gardening before I came here.

He topped up each of our wine glasses and placed the bottle back down, leaning his head back.

I gathered that fairly quickly.

A metallic strip smouldered over the mountain ridge. The fjord sparkled before us.

But I'm so sorry. If I had known how you felt about it, I...

He shook his head.

No. That was just what's called 'magical thinking' – what you do when you lose hope.

Even so.

No, Allis. Put that thought aside.

I drank slowly.

It's a beautiful night to stay up late, he said.

I want to stay up all night long, I replied.

Do you?

I do.

He stroked my back.

Are you cold?

No.

We heard the screeching of gulls in the distance. I closed my eyes. Listened to the sea. The wine warmed me from the inside out. Both the sky and the fjord were golden-yellow, like honey.

Shall I show you the beach? he asked all of a sudden.

The beach?

It's not far.

He stood up, offered me his hand and pulled me up with him. He walked out in front of me carrying the ice bucket, making his way behind the boathouse and clambering over the sloping coastal rocks. Be careful, he called down to me. I climbed up after him. The rocks had retained the warmth of the day's sun, dusty lilac sea thrift poking out between the cracks. We made our way along the rocky coastline, a light breeze blowing as he took my hand. After walking a few hundred metres south along the shoreline, the ground beneath us flattened out, a narrow strip of sand coming into view; it was high tide. I removed my sandals and walked on the warm sand, the sky above us orange, the grass beyond the sand a shade of blue.

It's so beautiful, I said, turning to face him. The breeze ruffled his hair. He walked with one hand in his pocket, carrying the bucket in the other, his skin almost black against the white of his shirt. What now? I thought. Is this how things are now, can they really be like this? Is this where I live? My life, the life that I'd considered to be as good as over just a year and a half ago, I had made work after all; I'd started afresh. Perhaps. Waves slipped gently over the sand, washing it clean. I hadn't believed it were possible. A large, white log rested on the sand. I stopped and sat down on it. He followed me. My skin tingled, goose bumps, I was sunburnt. It just felt good. Bagge's shoulder next to mine, the bucket in the sand between us. I brought the bottle to my lips, the melting ice inside the bucket causing it to drip, the wine cool as it trickled down my throat. I passed him the bottle and stroked the back of his neck, scratching him gently, running my hand through his hair. I was too happy to cry and too sad to smile. I didn't know what it was, I longed to feel light. For the very first time I was as good as free from any worries, and yet still my body existed in a state of suspense, perpetually on guard. The thought of him, believing or perhaps even knowing he felt the same way, yet without quite knowing why. Just the two of us, if it were even possible. I would need to pull myself together and call Johs sooner or later, sort things out between us. It was unbelievable that I'd put things off for this long, allowing matters to unfold as they had, tying me up in knots.

It's possible, he said, out of the blue.

What is?

This.

Do you think so?

Yes, Allis. I didn't at first, but I do now.

Are our best years ahead of us?

I think so.

Something erupted within my chest, I felt weightless. Then I heard him take a deep breath and let out a heavy sigh. He bowed his head.

Allis, I was considering doing something terrible. You saved me.

What do you mean?

He sat there, his face downturned.

What were you going to do?

At that moment a gull screeched just beside us and I jumped, looked up, watched as the bird dived at me, let out a howl and writhed out of the way, its beak snapping just by my ear before it soared upwards again just as quickly as it had swooped down. It was gone. Another squawk and it whizzed through the air, I ducked and felt something clawing at my hair before the bird rose up into the sky. Bagge leapt up and grabbed me by the arm. There were more of them now, and I shot up, pulled along behind him. Two gulls plunged in our direction, I screamed, the beating of a wing against my face, round eyes, beak, I crouched down low, he hauled me along after him.

Come on!

I held my free arm protectively across my face, the beating of wings in the air, running, stumbling, dashing across the beach with beaks snapping at my throat, then screeching, three gulls now, four, diving at us, white shapes hurtling towards Bagge. He hunched over to avoid them and we ran, gulls screaming like wild things, clawing at my hair, I gasped for air and wept in shock, feeling as if the world had been turned on its head as we scrambled over the beach, hastening flaps rushing through the air around us, sharp bills at our cheeks, tearing at skin as we scrambled back up onto the rock, sprinting away, stooped over, eyes squeezed shut for fear they'd pluck them out. More beating wings overwhelmed me, nipping at my ear, and I roared at them: Stop!

He pulled me in the direction of the forest, bare feet hurrying over grass and rocks, up towards the trees, sheltering from the screeching and clawing. We stopped. The gulls had gone.

He bent double and gulped for air.

Allis! I'm so sorry!

I looked up at him, my cheeks wet with tears and smeared with blood. He looked at me, his face filled with fear.

Did they get you?

Yes!

My God, Allis, let me see!

My chest burned as it rose and fell.

They were trying to kill me!

We got too close to their eggs, Allis.

I brought a hand to my ear, a stinging sensation, something wet against my fingertips.

They've never come so close before. Never. They usually just try to scare people away.

He wrapped an arm around me. He was pale.

We should go inside and see to your cuts.

I sobbed once, deeply, too worked up to break down in tears.

I've never seen anything like that, he said. They sometimes fly close to deter people from approaching their eggs or young, but I've never seen them actually attack anyone, ever.

I felt an overwhelming desire to destroy them, to learn to shoot. He held me close and walked me through the forest and back toward the house. There was silence all around us.

You're safe now.

Making our way out of the forest we walked down the bank to the house. The sky was crimson, the colour of blood. Inside I walked to the bathroom. The soles of my feet ached, I had bounded over rocks and branches to escape. I had left my sandals down on the beach. I washed my face, the wounds stinging. There was a small cut on my cheek from a claw, not quite as dramatic as it had first appeared, another cut at the top of my ear. It had stopped bleeding. I dried my face, looked at myself in the mirror. He stood behind me, his forehead wrinkled.

Could there be any risk of disease or infection from the cuts?

No, he said. I don't think so.

I looked at him in the mirror.

The thing you were about to say...

His gaze sank.

It's nothing.

You said it was terrible.

He shook his head behind me, backing out of the room.

I followed him.

He stood before me, his strong back under his light shirt. He turned to face me.

Allis. Shall we sit out on the veranda?

I nodded and pulled on the wool jumper I had left draped over the back of the chair by the kitchen table, following him outside.

It was cooler now. The sky was no longer red, but deep blue. The garden was dark, I could just see my vegetable patch, faintly illuminated in the weak moonlight. We kept the outside light off to avoid attracting insects. I sat in the chair beside him and exhaled deeply. Suddenly I started laughing.

My God, I said. You live in quite some place.

It's all my fault. Does it hurt?

No.

My cheek throbbed, but I wasn't in pain.

He'd had something that he had wanted to say, but now he didn't want to say anything after all. I didn't dare nag him about it, it took so little for him to clam up. There was nothing for it but to wait. Hunted by gulls, I thought, could anything be more degrading?

What happens next? Bagge asked quietly.

With us?

No, sorry, he said. I was thinking of something else. What happens to the gods, once Balder is dead and Loki is captured?

Were you thinking about that just now?

It's so wonderful to hear you tell the stories.

Well. Balder's death causes great unrest.

Oh?

Moral decay. Brothers fighting one another to the death. The dawning of *Ragnarök*. 'Völuspá', the first poem of the Poetic Edda, tells of the endless clashes between gods and evil forces, horrific scenes. The gods cease to exist. Odin is swallowed whole by the wolf Fenrir. Thor defeats the Midgard serpent, but is covered in the serpent's venom during the fight, which ultimately kills him.

Bagge sat in the darkness, listening closely.

The sun and stars turn black. The earth sinks into the sea. The world is submerged.

His chest stopped moving, he was holding his breath.

Then a new world emerges. The earth appears from the sea, green and new. Balder returns and lives in peace with his brother Höd. Loki is gone. Everything is beautiful. Even unsown fields abound with crops.

I stopped. Bagge was breathing once again.

There are no women in the new world, leaving it free from unrest and tension.

Clever.

Someone known as 'the Mighty One' comes from above. He turns up at the court of law, settles matters and writes laws. Old guilt is destroyed by fire and swallowed by the sea.

What does that mean?

Well, I said. Perhaps it means that guilt requires atonement, perhaps it needs to be wiped out if a new world is to emerge?

So everything is good again?

Not quite. The very last verse of 'Völuspá' tells of the dragon Nithhogg, who sweeps through the air from Nithafjoll and into the new world with human corpses nestled among its feathers. That's where it ends.

I turned to Bagge and he regarded me gravely.

What does it all mean?

I don't know, I said. Maybe that even in the new world there is potential for evil.

He sat with his head bowed then looked up at me suddenly, swiftly.

There's something I need to tell you.

He rubbed his hands up and down his thighs.

Because I want to be completely honest with you. If we're to start afresh.

Wait, I said. I need to tell you something first.

He held up a hand.

No, hear me out. He took a deep breath. You need to know.

What?

About that day. Out on the fjord.

A shudder ran through me as he said the words.

Yes, I said. The accident.

Yes. He turned to face me. But it wasn't like that.

He looked at me, his eyes two dark hollows, glimmering faintly.

We sat there that night, wrapped in a blanket, the fire burning brightly, speaking in hushed tones, never growing tired.

He looked away from me, gazing outwards.

It was completely dark, just as it is now. And then it grew light again.

He bit his lip.

Conditions were tropical that night. We stayed there until the break of day, then we pushed the boat out onto the water. We grabbed a fishing rod and staggered into the boat, I can remember the sound of her laughter just behind me.

You've already told me all of this, I said, relieved.

He took no notice of me, ploughing ahead with his account.

She rowed. She loved to row, her arms were strong and each stroke of the oar was long and slow. Outside of the boat, everything was calm, the sun beginning to emerge over the mountain ridge. I cast out and let the spinner follow the boat. The fjord glittered, the sky was perfectly clear. We rowed out to the middle of the fjord. I felt the high slowly subside, sitting at the back of the boat and watching her there before me, clear as day. How beautiful she was. She rowed slowly, smoothly, her gaze turned downwards, appearing to be in her own little world. I felt so calm, so happy. Her cheeks glowed in the morning light. The air was crisp and clear, fresh. The birds tweeted.

He stopped. It was pitch black all around us now, the night at its darkest point.

I told her I loved her. She looked up at me and there were tears running down her face. At first I thought she was happy.

I felt my pulse thumping in my stomach, wanted to hear about her and yet didn't.

She wept silently and looked away from me, almost seeming to look over her shoulder, but still she rowed, weeping softly all the while. Nor, I said. What is it? She said nothing. What is it? She took a deep breath, sighed. She tried to dry her tears on her shoulders, still rowing all the while.

Bagge's voice was hushed, sombre.

She looked at me and replied: I'm in mourning. You're in mourning? I repeated, almost relieved. She nodded and looked down. What are you in mourning for? She said nothing. Nor, I said. What are you in mourning for? She started crying again. Can you talk to me about it? She shook her head. Why not?

He paused for breath. His eyes were closed and his brow furrowed, his expression solemn, just as it was when he made love, as if he felt everything, every feeling, good and bad, all at once.

I felt such tenderness for her. Have you lost someone? I heard a choking sound, then she wept silently again. Nor, my love, I said. Is it someone from the orchestra? I heard a faint hiccup from deep down, a yes. Recently? I asked. She said nothing. My love, I repeated. She wouldn't meet my gaze. Will you be going to the funeral? She shook her head. I thought about how small she seemed, like a little girl. I said no more. She had stopped rowing. She sat there with the oars in her lap and gazed down. You poor thing, I said. Losing someone like that. The entire sun had risen behind the mountain by this point, my skin tingled. When was this? I asked her. Her upper body collapsed, she bowed her head. A year ago, she said. It pained me to hear her say it. She had carried the burden of a loss I had no notion of, a loss she still thought about. What did it mean? She was no longer crying. Why didn't you say anything? You lovely thing. She gazed vacantly into the distance. I couldn't grieve. Why not? I couldn't. But Nor, why couldn't you? She pressed her lips together, didn't want to say another word. He... she began, but pressed her lips together once again.

He paused for a few moments. I didn't dare look at him, felt my breath catch in my throat, didn't want to make a single sound.

I knew then what it meant. I asked what had happened. He fell ill, Nor said. Did you look after him? No, his family looked after him. Was he married? She nodded. Did it go on for long, you and him? She nodded slowly.

His jaw was clenched as he spoke, tense.

She looked up: But I was never going to leave you! Suddenly I saw her clearly; she was ugly, her face distorted. She wanted me to comfort her. She wanted *me* to comfort *her*! And my body leapt up to grab her, and the fishing rod fell in the water, and the boat rocked as she jumped back to get away, the oars sliding out of her grasp, and she fell back – everything happened so quickly, and suddenly I was standing in the boat, calmly, waiting for her, quivering with anger, and she was under, deep down in the black depths, and I dived in, but I couldn't see her, had to come up for air again and again, and then eventually I saw her deep down beneath me, pulled her up to the surface, but it was too late.

Couldn't she swim? I whispered.

They later found out that she'd hit the back of her head on the gunwale.

We sat in silence. I was afraid of him. He had this in him.

What happened after that?

Then there was the hospital, and after that, when they realised there wasn't anything they could do, the nursing home. And then – I stopped visiting her.

Why?

He gave no reply.

Why didn't you visit her?

I couldn't bear to look at her.

So she was conscious?

No. No. But I just couldn't.

Was she completely...

Brain-dead. Yes.

He closed his eyes. I leaned my head back and looked up at the dark sky. He was leagues ahead of me in the suffering stakes, and I had no idea what help it could be to have me there, a nuisance who took an immaturely joyful approach to everything. I had nothing to offer but a hot meal and warm skin. Everything that it occurred to me to say to him was worthless. He seemed ashamed. I wanted to assure him that he shouldn't be. He didn't need to be.

Thank you for telling me, I eventually muttered.

He turned to face me, his eyes gleaming. He rested his head in his hands, his shoulders high, making no sound. I moved my chair closer to his, placing an arm around him. I brought my lips to his ear.

Things will be all right.

He sat there in silence, not trembling, not shedding a single tear, just sitting there.

Things will be all right, I said again.

He removed his hands from his face and wrapped his arms around me. He held me tight as I stroked his back. I tried to process all that he had told me, to imagine living with this. His life viewed through this lens suddenly made sense. Living this way, dreaming as he did. His body was warm against mine. A cricket chirruped intensely, its song piercing the still of the night. We sat unmoving in the grey light as I gripped tightly onto the flimsy, light material of his shirt, his dark hair soft against my cheek. I felt his heart beating against my breast, a fast, even thudding. I took a deep breath and stroked his head. I took his face in my hands and rested my forehead against his.

Things will be all right.

He was quiet. Kissed both of my eyelids.

Allis, he whispered. I have something for you.

Something for me?

He nodded, then stood up and stretched an arm out towards me. I took his hand and he pulled me out of my chair.

What is it?

You'll see.

All of a sudden he seemed cheerful, enigmatic, slipping an arm around my waist and leading me down into the garden. I walked barefoot through the grass, damp with the humidity of the night. The fruit trees were grey and knotted against the brightening sky.

All the way down, he whispered, nudging me ahead of him down the stone steps. Slowly I descended, tense, the soles of my feet against the cold, hard stone. The landscape was peaceful in the morning gloom, the fjord black.

Wait here, he said when we were standing on the jetty. And don't look. He held my shoulders in his hands and twirled me around so that I was facing the steps. There was a mild, cool breeze in the air and as I stared straight ahead, a quiver surged through me. I heard him pull open the side door of the boathouse, the hinges creaking.

Stay there, he said. I nodded. I heard the sound of material being pulled away, short bursts of sweeping.

Allis.

Yes?

His voice was gruff. I thought about the time I had spent here. Walking down the drive for the first time, early that April, what could I have been thinking as I neared the house? I had alighted at the bus stop by the main road, everything that I owned packed into two bags. And there was Sigurd, with his dark hair, his shirts, his long strides. So strange to think back on it all now.

You can turn around.

Those first months. So difficult to bear; he'd been so hard on me. I'd been so weak. Was it me who had changed since then, or just my circumstances?

I turned around. The door to the boathouse was open. There stood Sigurd in the half-darkness. He stepped to one side. On the floor of the boathouse behind him was a bright, shining wooden boat; it filled the entire space. I saw straight away that it was an *Oselvar*, a beautiful, curved, wooden *færing*. I stood there, open-mouthed. Looked at Sigurd. He smiled inquisitively. I took a few steps forward.

Did you build this?

He nodded.

By yourself?

Yes.

I walked inside and placed a hand on the gunwale, letting it glide along the smooth timber, the rowlock. I turned to look at him.

Is this what you've been working on?

He nodded again.

I circled the boat slowly.

It's so beautiful.

Sigurd looked at me, peaceful, content.

I made it for you.

I stopped, looked at him.

For me?

Yes. It's yours.

No.

Yes.

I looked at the boat. It was perfect. I didn't know what to say, how to show him just how overwhelmed I was.

It must have taken such a long time.

Yes, it's been a while.

I suddenly felt so proud, proud that I was his. This was a man who could build a boat. When you can build a boat all by yourself, there are no limits to what you can do.

Have you tried it out on the fjord?

Not yet.

Though I'd been up all night, I felt strangely wide awake. The sky was growing ever brighter. It wouldn't be long before the sun would rise from behind the forest.

Can we put it in the water?

Now?

Yes?

Would you like to?

I really would.

He looked as if he were thinking things over for a moment.

Yes. Of course we can, he said. If you help me.

He walked over and opened the doors wide onto the fjord. The water was still. He placed the oars inside the boat and we lifted it carefully from the small wooden frame it had been sitting on. It was heavy, our knuckles turning white as we carried it over to the boat landing and placed it down. We let it slide down the thick planks of wood towards the shallows. I crept barefoot over the stones and down to the water's edge.

Hop in, he said.

I climbed into the boat. Sigurd removed his shoes and rolled up his trousers. He pushed the boat down the boat landing until it was in the water. He climbed over the gunwale and perched himself on the thwart opposite me. I used one of the oars to push us out. The boat was floating on the water now. Slowly we drifted further out. The fjord was breathlessly still. The sky grew lighter and lighter, not a sound to be heard besides the lively chirping from the forest. Sigurd held out his hands for the oars.

Can I row? I asked. I love to row.

He looked at me.

Of course, Allis. It's your boat.

I slotted the oars into the rowlocks, took hold and pulled. We darted across the water.

I can't believe it. To think that you can build something so beautiful.

He gave a warm smile.

Feel how beautifully it sits in the water.

He nodded.

Have you done this before?

He looked at me.

Yes.

Slowly I rowed us out, the previous night's high beginning to lift. I felt completely awake. It was such a mild morning, so clear. The fjord was so still. Sigurd sat with a peaceful expression on his face and looked out over the water. With each stroke of the oars, the breeze ruffled his hair. A wake followed the boat over the fjord, sweeping across the surface and leading all the way back to the boathouse. The house looked so small from all the way out here. The garden, too. So many stories and events were contained within the image I had before me. That first bottle of wine shared under the cherry tree. Sigurd lying in the grass in the rain. The birds in the traps.

I could see the beach from the boat, a narrow, pale strip of land only a short distance from the boathouse. The log we had sat on. Our escape route over the rocky coastline and up into the forest. When the gulls swooped in, just as they arrived, what was it that he had said? I couldn't recall, but I felt something heavy in my chest at the mere thought. That he had – that I had saved him? From what? His grief for Nor? No. Something else. Saved him from something he was going to do. Something terrible.

A strip of sunlight emerged behind the forest at that moment and stung my eyes, forging a sudden bright outline around Sigurd. The surface of the dark fjord glimmered.

Look, I said. My sandals, there on the beach. I nodded towards land. He turned to look back over one shoulder.

Where?

By the log, where we sat.

He nodded. I see them.

I hesitated for a moment.

When we were sitting there. The thing you were about to say, right before the birds came.

He turned to face me again.

What?

You were in the middle of telling me something.

He stared at me, looking as if he were trying to recapture something, recall a memory.

You said I had saved you, I continued, a beam of sunshine hitting my face. I gazed at him, squinting in the sunlight.

He shook his head gently.

From something you'd been thinking of doing.

I could see that he knew, he was feigning ignorance. I rowed out with slow, steady strokes.

Something terrible.

He nodded, holding my gaze. Yes, he said. I know. But it doesn't matter anymore.

But what was it?

He paused. I saw him take a deep breath.

Allis. No.

Yes.

Only if you promise that you won't go around thinking about it afterwards.

I nodded.

I promise.

We glided slowly across the water. I let the oars sit in the rowlocks, drops falling from them, down and into the water.

The boat, he said. I started building it before you came.

I thought so.

Right after burning the other one.

He looked up at me, something apologetic about the way he fur-rowed his brows.

I had decided that if Nor were ever to wake up, then — that if she weren't to wake up, if she were to die, then I would row out, and—

Don't say it, I whispered.

And I would drown myself.

He looked down.

Something in me wound itself tight.

I had it all planned. I'd thought about it for so long.

Don't say any more.

I was going to row out to the middle of the fjord with the anvil tied to one leg.

But ... why? My voice was barely audible.

He said nothing.

It wasn't your fault.

He sat there, his head bowed. The oars were no longer dripping. My arms were limp.

Because... he began. I don't know. Because I wanted to.

I couldn't say a thing, was just aware of the way we floated on the water, bobbing almost unnoticeably.

But you promised me, Allis. It was a long time ago. Everything is different now.

When did you change your mind?

A long time ago.

When?

I don't know.

He looked at me imploringly.

Don't think about it. You promised me you wouldn't.

I nodded slowly. My chest ached, it was hard to breathe. This was bigger than I had thought it would be. The guilt he felt about the accident. It would always be there. Always. He would never be free. I didn't dare look at him. If only that day could be erased. Perhaps I had saved him from taking the boat out to end things, but he could never be saved from the sorrow that had made him consider doing it to begin with. That would remain with him forever. I began rowing again.

Don't think about it.

No.

I could see it so clearly now, here in the boat, the dark sea below us, I could see it all. Diving down, searching, up for air then down again, over and over, hope diminishing with each dive.

He sat straddle-legged on the thwart, his feet bare, gazing out across the fjord, the sun on his back, his face creased. I had saved him. It didn't feel that way. I didn't really believe that it felt that way for him, either. If anything, it had been him that had saved me by placing his bizarre ad, extricating me from everything.

It was Nanna, he said. Balder's wife. After you told me about her, it was impossible. I couldn't do anything that might hurt you.

Do you mean that?

Yes.

My gaze swept out across the water. We had almost reached the middle of the fjord. It was a long way to land, the house no more than a speck on the horizon. The sky was pale yellow and light blue, the fjord inconceivably, sparklingly beautiful. He had never seen me swim. Instantly it hit me. He didn't know that I could. If he could save me here, out in the fjord, save my life, if I could appear to be helpless, then everything would be reversed. Perhaps then he'd be free.

A moment ago... I began.

He turned to look at me.

What you told me before.

Yes?

I have something too, I whispered. Something to tell you. So we can start afresh.

His brow furrowed slightly.

It's not all that important. But I still want you to know.

The silence and the morning light, the glistening fjord, it all made everything seem so much greater than I had first thought it to be.

I should have told you much earlier, but it just didn't occur to me.

What?

I could tell from his tone that he was anxious.

But then one day I realised that you asked me, a long time ago. And I don't know why, but I wasn't honest with you then.

I heard him stop breathing. I pulled the oars up out of the water and rested them across my lap.

It's just that...

Oh, Allis, I thought to myself.

... the formalities haven't been dealt with quite yet.

He said nothing. The thing he had told me about Nor that night. About the man who fell ill. I took a deep breath.

But I was actually married when I came here.

I dropped my gaze as I spoke.

And so ... I still am. Married, that is.

He was silent. I looked down, waiting for him to say something.

But it's not important.

He said nothing. We bobbed warily on the fjord.

All my life I've been slow at dealing with practical things, I said, the words ringing hollow.

But the reason that I haven't done anything, it's just that the whole thing means so little to me. Since meeting you, I mean.

My heart was beating harder than I had anticipated.

Won't you say something, please?

I looked up at him. He sat in silence, staring straight past me.

Sigurd?

His cheekbones, the dark hollows of his eyes, his sunken cheeks, something brutal had come over him.

Hello?

I waved a hand.

Please, say something.

I was about to reach out to touch his knee, but all of a sudden I didn't dare.

I understand that I've devalued its meaning. I'm sorry.

I looked at him.

But please, won't you say something? Anything?

His expression was unchanging. He didn't blink. His breathing was even as he stared into the distance.

Sigurd?

Another one.

What did you say?

He looked me in the eye.

You're just another one.

Just another what?

Yes, he said, inhaling sharply. The corners of his mouth curled upwards ever so slightly.

What do you mean?

He shook his head slowly. The cool morning air gave me goose bumps. He said nothing else. I waited. Inwardly I had really believed that it didn't matter. I couldn't see that it did, either.

Tell me what's wrong, I said.

He was silent, his eyes fixed on the horizon.

Is it that I was unfaithful? I asked.

He turned around sharply.

Yes.

He held my gaze. His eyes were black.

To you?

To him.

But what does it matter?

I can't trust you.

Yes! Yes, you can.

No.

He shook his head.

Yes. Always.

His gaze didn't waver. He stared at me, his eyes shining.

Trust me, I whispered. I gazed at him imploringly.

They can't destroy what we have. Nobody can.

They, he said. There's nobody here but us. You're laying the blame elsewhere, Allis.

OK, me, I said. *I* won't destroy what we have. I promise.

Suddenly he reached around and grasped the hair at the back of my head in one hand, gripping it tightly.

You promise the same thing to everyone, he hissed, teeth clenched.

No, I whispered, forcing the sound out, not anymore.

I felt stinging at the nape of my neck. He tightened his grip.

What do you want me to say? I whispered.

He gave no reply.

What do you want me to do?

He said nothing. Just held my gaze. The boat rocked. I had lost any feeling I had once had at the back of my head, I no longer felt any pain, only his fist, his tight grip. I could do it now. I could tear myself away, fall overboard, let him save me. We'd get what we wanted most. The old world would sink into the sea, a new one rising from the deep. The sun's bright orb had emerged proudly from behind the forest, soaring high into the sky, prickling my face. His expression, his hand. I had to fall over the gunwale, I had to be helpless. I heard the sound of my breathing, shallow gasps. I turned my gaze to the water. It was so still, so clear. The sun. The surface of the water reflected the shining-bright woodwork. The oars were long and pale, the sky blue. The fjord was green and bright, sunbeams penetrating the water's surface, breaking through and extending several metres underwater. Our boat. Built for starting afresh. I readied myself to break free from his grasp, to meet the surface of the water, break through it, sink beneath it, to force myself not to swim, to let him save himself by saving me. I took a deep breath, closed my eyes. I prepared to pull away, out of his grasp, to tumble overboard. Gulls circled overhead. It was all so strange.

Didn't you tell me, I whispered, that the water was black?

He said nothing.

It was sunrise. That's what you told me last night.

I locked eyes with him, my neck stiff.

The sea isn't black.

I took a deep breath.

What really happened?

He gave no answer. Ashen alarm swept across his face, his breathing shallow. He looked at me darkly.

What happened?

He closed his eyes, saying nothing.

I felt something erupt within me, forced to gasp for air.

When she fell overboard, I said.

He looked at me keenly, my hair still in his clenched fist.

It can't have been difficult to see her.

He said nothing.

It can't have been difficult to reach her, to pull her up to the surface.

I felt a cold sweat forming as I held his gaze.

Did she fall?

His breathing was shallow, panicked, he said nothing.

*Nithing*, I thought. All of a sudden he looked grotesque, his face distorted. A carnivore. I had to save myself.

I wasn't able to break free before he leapt at me, grabbing both of my wrists. The oars slipped from my grasp and slid down into the water. Gulls screeched overhead. The boat rocked, seawater sloshing in over the gunwale. He was too strong. I fell back over the thwart, the wind knocked out of me, the back of my head slamming against the prow. He pushed down on top of me, his body heavy. Saltwater stung my eyes. He pressed his lips hard against mine. I clenched my teeth and bit hard, gnashing at flesh. He leapt back with a roar, red streaming from his mouth. Eyes as black as coal. I plunged an arm into the water. My fingertips grazed the oar. So heavy. Every wheezing gasp for air tore at my throat. He lunged at me, his hands, I heaved and swung my upper body around with a scream, a sharp whack above the eye. A loud splash. Then everything fell silent.

The taste of salt and blood in my mouth. I rolled onto my side with a gasp, arms and legs trembling, then clambered onto my knees and lay slumped over the thwart. Hacking coughs, I gasped for air. The boat rocked. The fjord glittered in the morning light. I peered over the gunwale. Light shirt, black hair, he was there, just beneath the surface. His rough brown hands, pallid underwater. My chest heaved. I stared wide-eyed into the depths. His hair was exquisite in the water, dancing from side to side. His dark forehead, his shirt almost transparent. His eyes were closed, not looking at me.

I couldn't tear my gaze from his hair, swirling underwater, a million fine, whirling fibres. I dipped an arm beneath the surface, the dark wisps brushing my hand, each one tenderly stroking it. I wanted to grasp at it, but it slipped between my fingers and was pulled down, down, sinking to depths out of reach of the sunbeams. After that, the fjord was simply green. A pair of wings circled in the sky above me. I looked up, a dark shadow with corpses nestled among its feathers.

FREEDOM
TO **WRITE**
FREEDOM
TO **READ**

This book has been selected to receive financial assistance from English PEN's Writers in Translation programme supported by Bloomberg and Arts Council England. English PEN exists to promote literature and its understanding, uphold writers' freedoms around the world, campaign against the persecution and imprisonment of writers for stating their views, and promote the friendly co-operation of writers and free exchange of ideas.

Each year, a dedicated committee of professionals selects books that are translated into English from a wide variety of foreign languages. We award grants to UK publishers to help translate, promote, market and champion these titles. Our aim is to celebrate books of outstanding literary quality, which have a clear link to the PEN charter and promote free speech and intercultural understanding.

In 2011, Writers in Translation's outstanding work and contribution to diversity in the UK literary scene was recognised by Arts Council England. English PEN was awarded a threefold increase in funding to develop its support for world writing in translation.

*www.englishpen.org*